OH BROTHER!

As the only girl in the family, Stevie often found herself grouped with her three brothers. Most of the time she didn't mind that. In fact, she usually enjoyed herself when they all got into something like touch football or Frisbee. But she was also proud of the things she did by herself.

Riding was Number One.

There was no way she wanted her older brother Chad at Pine Hollow—it was *hers*. He didn't belong there. But if her parents insisted that Chad be allowed to learn to ride, she had only one recourse. She would completely, absolutely, one hundred percent ignore him.

She reached for the phone, eager for the comfort of Carole's voice.

"Guess what," Stevie began mournfully. "All of a sudden, Chad has decided that he wants to learn to ride. Mom has already signed him up for riding camp. Can you believe it? Dumb old Chad is going to be at Pine Hollow every single day!"

"I know he's your brother and all, Stevie," Carole said. "But he's really not all that bad. Remember when we were having a Saddle Club meeting at your house and he brought us cookies and milk?"

"Okay, so once in his fourteen years, he wasn't a total doofus," Stevie conceded graciously.

Carole could barely stifle her giggles. "Don't worry, Lisa and I will be there to protect you. Give him a chance, will you?"

"One," Stevie agreed. "But the first time he makes a fool of himself, I'm going to disown him!"

Bantam Books in THE SADDLE CLUB series. Ask your bookseller for the books you have missed:

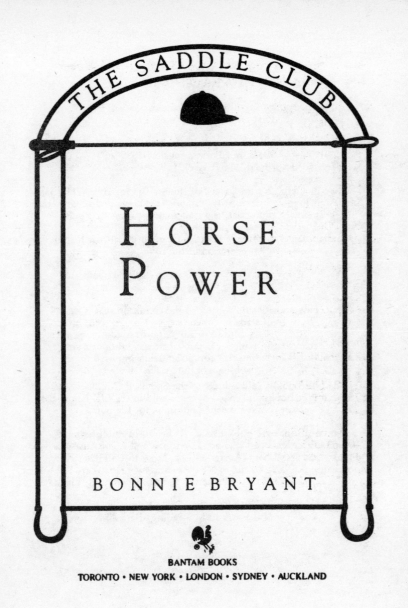

THE SADDLE CLUB

HORSE POWER

BONNIE BRYANT

BANTAM BOOKS
TORONTO • NEW YORK • LONDON • SYDNEY • AUCKLAND

THE SADDLE CLUB: HORSE POWER
A BANTAM BOOK 0 553 17653 6

First published in USA by Bantam Skylark Books
First publication in Great Britain

PRINTING HISTORY
Bantam edition published 1989
Reprinted 1990 (twice), 1991, 1992, 1993

Bantam Books are published by Transworld Publishers Ltd.,
61–63 Uxbridge Road, Ealing, London W5 5SA, in Australia by
Transworld Publishers (Australia) Pty. Ltd., 15–25 Helles Avenue,
Moorebank, NSW 2170, and in New Zealand by Transworld Publishers
(N.Z.) Ltd., 3 William Pickering Drive, Albany, Auckland.

Printed and bound in Great Britain by
Cox & Wyman Ltd., Reading, Berkshire

—for Neil

"IT'S THREE WEEKS from today exactly, right?" Stevie Lake asked, propping her chin on the palm of her hand. She was stretched out comfortably on the floor in Carole Hanson's room. Carole was sitting cross-legged on her bed. Lisa Atwood, the third member of the trio who called themselves The Saddle Club, sat in the sunny window seat, stroking Carole's kitten, Snowball.

"Exactly three weeks until the gymkhana," Lisa confirmed. "In fact, the first game will probably start about four o'clock, so that's three weeks, minus one hour and twenty-five minutes."

Carole and Stevie laughed. "Trust you to be so precise," Stevie teased.

"I'm not always all that precise," Lisa said, smiling.

"Just when I'm really looking forward to something. . . ."

"Then you count the hours, right?" Carole asked.

"Yes, and in this case, it's—" She paused, grinning mischievously. "Oh, golly, just about five hundred and two and a half hours, give or take five minutes." All three girls giggled. Lisa was known for being a straight-A student, but sometimes even she had to admit she carried it to extremes.

A gymkhana was a series of games and relay races in which teams of young riders competed on horseback. This particular gymkhana was to take place at Pine Hollow Stables, where all three girls rode. Any gymkhana would be fun, but this one was certain to be especially so because Stevie, Lisa, and Carole were all planning the games together. They had been working for weeks to come up with appropriately outrageous stunts the riders would have to perform.

The three girls made an unusual trio. They agreed among themselves that the only things they really had in common were their love of horses and their friendship with one another. In fact, the Club's only rules were that members had to be horse crazy, and willing to help other members. The Club's first joint project had been to help Stevie with a math project. Its most recent effort had been to make up games for the gymkhana.

Carole, at twelve, was the most experienced rider of the three. She had been raised on various Marine

Corps bases where her father, a colonel, had been stationed. They had moved a lot as his assignments had changed. Until her father had bought the house where they now lived in Willow Creek, Virginia, she had usually ridden on the bases. Now she rode at Pine Hollow, owned and operated by Max Regnery, the girls' beloved instructor.

Carole had wavy black hair, which fell softly to her shoulders. She had a gentle voice and an easy smile. Since her mother's death the year before, a lot of things had been difficult and uncertain for Carole. But the one thing she knew for sure was that horses were very important to her. Carole was determined to ride them, train them, tend them, and own them for the rest of her life. Carole could sometimes be forgetful or disorganized, but when it came to horses, her friends thought she was the most organized person in the world.

"You know, I can't wait for the gymkhana either," Carole said. "But just think how great it'll be when we're old enough, and good enough, to ride in the *real* thing. I mean real horse shows where—"

"I'll never get that good," Lisa groaned. "I just can't picture myself competing at Madison Square Garden in New York, can you?"

"You mean, can I see you or *me?*" Carole joked. "I can see me, that's for sure. That's my dream—at least one of my dreams," she said. "Sometimes I try to imagine what it would be like. I read about it, too. But I don't think the magazine stories are anything like the real thing."

"Make you a deal," Stevie said to Carole. "If you get to ride in the Horse Show at Madison Square Garden, Lisa and I will be there in the audience to cheer you on. It's a promise." Stevie pulled herself up into a sitting position and reached across the bed to shake Carole's hand.

Like Carole, Stevie was twelve. Although she came from a comfortably wealthy ramily, she didn't dress like it. In fact, Lisa teased her sometimes, saying she didn't know if Stevie owned anything but jeans. The first time she'd been to Stevie's room, she'd threatened to look through her closet to check. But the closet was such a mess when she opened the door, she didn't dare touch anything for fear of causing an avalanche!

Stevie had dark blond hair and blue eyes that sparkled with mischief. She was never far from hot water—and frequently in it. She was a practical joker with a wild sense of humor and a streak of stubbornness. Stevie had three brothers—one older, one younger, and one twin. She was the only member of her family who rode horses, and she liked it that way. Riding was one thing that made her special in her family.

Lisa Atwood, at thirteen, was the oldest of the three girls, but hardly looked it. She usually wore classic styles, such as kilts and loafers, which, along with her long wavy brown hair and her sweet smile, made her appear several years younger than her friends. She was also the newest at horseback riding, having taken it up only a few months before. Her mother, who had very firm ideas of what her daughter should do to be a proper young lady, had decided Lisa should learn something about horses because "every well-bred woman should." Lisa hadn't agreed at all. She'd been very frightened at the start, but she'd been more intimidated by her mother than by the horses, so she'd reluctantly agreed to lessons. Then, once she'd tried riding, she'd changed her mind and discovered that she not only liked riding, but *loved* it.

That wasn't what her mother had had in mind at all. As Lisa learned more and more about horses and riding, she became more confident, and finally convinced her mother to let her drop painting, ballet, and the miscellaneous music lessons that made a well-bred young lady—at least for the summer. Now that it was summer, all three of the girls were in Pine Hollow's riding-camp program, which met every weekday from nine to three. The summer was going to culminate in a three-day event for the adult riders at the stable, and a three-day gymkhana for the junior riders, including The Saddle Club members.

"You know, I can't wait to see how the costume race goes," Stevie said. "I hope our team gets the clown costume. It's just one piece—"

"Yeah, with buttons down the back!" Lisa reminded her. "And anyway, what makes you think we'll be on the same team? I'm sure Max is going to want to have riders of all ages on each team."

"It's not really age that will matter," Carole said sensibly. "It's more a matter of equal riding skills. Each team should have one very experienced rider, one moderately so, one pretty new rider, and, uh—" Carole paused, searching for the right word.

"One hopelessly new one?" Stevie said.

"Something like that," Carole said, laughing.

"Speaking of our events, are we going to have practice tomorrow?" Lisa asked.

"I can't," Carole said with regret. "Dad's got this plan to meet with an old Marine Corps buddy and his wife. They've got a daughter about my age and Dad is just sure we're going to get along famously."

"Don't you hate it when parents do that?" Stevie asked. "The last time mine said something like that, the girl was, first of all, nine years old, and second of all, this incredible brat."

"Maybe Carole will get lucky," Lisa said. She always tried to look on the bright side of things.

"It can't be all that bad," Carole said. "We're meeting them at Quantico, the big Marine Corps base where we used to live, and at least I'll have a chance to visit the stables there. We're going to have a cookout overlooking the reservoir, so even if she's a nine-year-old brat, it should be fun."

"What an optimist!" Stevie joked. "Oh, and speaking of optimists," Stevie said, changing the subject, "my brother Chad has been behaving very strangely lately."

"Why do you call him an optimist?" Lisa asked.

"Oh, because it's like he's just discovered *girls* and all he wants to think about is *girls,* and he's just positive that all the *girls* in the world are crazy about him. Considering his table manners, he'll be lucky to get a date by the time he's twenty-five!"

"You're always complaining about your brothers, Stevie," Lisa said, "but you don't know how rough it can be being an only child."

"I know, I know," Stevie said. "I just wish I had a couple of sisters instead of all those brothers. They can be real jerks sometimes."

"Oh, come on, Stevie," Carole said. "I know some girls who think Chad's kind of cute."

"Boy, they must be desperate." Stevie groaned.

"Who's desperate?" Colonel Hanson asked, knocking lightly on the jamb and entering the open door to Carole's room.

"Any girl interested in my brother," Stevie explained.

Colonel Hanson smiled at her. "I think my sister used to say that about me, too," he said. "Until I married her best friend!"

"Aw, no way, Dad," Carole protested. "Nobody could ever call you a dweeb." She gazed affectionately at her father. They had always been close, but the year since her mother's death had brought them even closer.

"Well, I don't know that *that's* the word they'd use,

but there are a couple of junior officers over at the base
. . ." The girls looked at him and giggled. "And speaking of the base, Carole, you and I have to put together
our barbecue stuff for the picnic tomorrow. So, Stevie
and Lisa, I'm afraid it's time for me to drive you
home—otherwise I'll have to start charging your parents for rent."

"I don't know about the Atwoods, but I think my
parents would let me stay for free," Stevie said.

"Very funny," Colonel Hanson returned. "Come
on."

Lisa sat up, trying to remove the kitten from her lap.
"Come on, Snowball," she told the little bundle of
black fur. "Time to get up. I'm going home now." The
kitten ignored her. He tucked his nose under a paw
and shut his eyes even more tightly.

"You should know Snowball better than that by
now," Carole told her.

"Oh, yeah, right," Lisa said, remembering why the
black kitten was named Snowball. He had a way of
doing the exact opposite of what anybody told him.
Lisa stroked his soft back gently. "There, there, Snowball. Just sleep tight," she said in a warm, comforting
voice. The kitten's head perked up. He looked at Lisa
with disdain, rose abruptly, stretched briefly, and
marched off her lap. Lisa shook her head in amaze-
ment. "Just like magic."

THERE WAS SOMETHING about Kate Devine that immediately told Carole they were going to be friends.

"Hi, you must be Carole," Kate said, grinning broadly. "My parents have been telling me how much I'm going to like you."

Carole laughed. "Same here," she said, admiring Kate's easy manner. The two of them were walking together toward the shore of the Quantico reservoir next to the picnic area while their fathers hashed over old times and tried to start the barbecue fire in the grill.

"The last time my parents guaranteed I was going to like an 'old friend's' daughter, it turned out to be a son," Kate confided.

"Cute?" Carole asked, curious.

"Very cute," Kate assured her. "Most two-year-olds are, you know!"

They giggled together, sitting down by the water's edge. "Well, I guess this time, our parents were right, so that's one for them," Carole said.

"Now, the next big test is, can those guys start the fire for the barbecue?" Kate said.

"They're both Marines," Carole reminded her. "They ought to be able to handle that."

"Dad told me a story once about a test he had in a Marine school course he took," Kate said. "There was a question about how an officer should start a fire if he or she didn't have any matches. Dad wrote this big-deal essay about lenses, spontaneous combustion, rubbing sticks together, and so on."

"So he got the answer right?"

"Nope," Kate said. "The correct answer was that an officer should say: 'Sergeant, come on over here and start this fire.'"

"I think the woman at the next campsite is a sergeant," Carole said, still laughing. "So we'll be okay, but it might take awhile. Have you had the grand tour of the base yet?" she asked.

"We've only been here three days," Kate told her. "And it's so big—there's so much to see. You used to live here, didn't you?"

"Yes, until two years ago. But even when you live here, there's a lot you never get to. One place I always got to, though, was the stable. Have you been there?"

"No," Kate said simply.

Carole was a little surprised that Kate didn't seem to show any interest in the stable. She didn't ask where it was, or if she rode there, or anything. Just no. Carole decided to pursue the subject.

"Would you like to see it?" she asked.

Kate hesitated. She seemed to be searching for her answer. As far as Carole was concerned, there were only two kinds of people in the world: those who were horse crazy and those who were just plain crazy. Kate didn't strike her as just plain crazy, so she waited for her answer.

"Oh, maybe later," Kate said noncommittally.

Carole made up her mind immediately that she'd introduce Kate to horses. If Kate was going to be a friend, that would be the nicest thing Carole could possibly share with her. She smiled to herself, thinking what a treat she had in store for Kate.

"Say, I love that sweater of yours," Kate said, changing the subject. "It's a really pretty color."

"Oh, thanks. Dad gave it to me for my birthday. He's got great taste. . . ."

"Speaking of dads and great taste," Kate said, "unless my nose deceives me, the fire's going and our fathers are already cooking. Look at my dad in that apron, will you?"

Carole glanced over at Colonel Devine. He had donned a giant chef's hat and apron and was brandishing a long-handled spatula, apparently threatening a hamburger with it.

"Maybe we'd better get back there and see if we can help—at least to save our own dinners!"

A few minutes later, the Devines and the Hansons were assembled at a picnic table. Mrs. Devine had brought everything to make it all look picture-perfect. There was a red-and-white-checked tablecloth, matching plates, napkins, even salt and pepper shakers.

"Phyllis, you're so organized!" Colonel Hanson said, admiring her handiwork. "I bet you've got everything unpacked—and flowers on the table already, right?"

Mrs. Devine laughed in protest. "No, I'm not all that organized. Besides, I don't know where we'll finally settle. For now, we're just in the family suites at Liversedge."

"Well, if you want to buy a home nearby, I'd be glad to show you around Willow Creek," Colonel Hanson offered. "It's a lovely town. Carole and I are very happy there," he added.

Carole was suddenly excited by the idea that Kate might live nearby. She would teach Kate to ride at Pine Hollow. They'd go to school together. Kate could even join The Saddle Club! "That would be great," she said to Kate. "We could spend a lot of time together. Oh, please, do come look at Willow Creek," she told the Devines.

Mrs. Devine looked at the girls quickly, knitting her brows ever so slightly. Then, as Carole watched, Colonel and Mrs. Devine exchanged glances. The colonel finally said, "Well, that's very nice of you to offer, Mitch, but we're—well, our plans are a little up in the air."

It had seemed such a simple question, but the responses told Carole that something was up, and the Devines weren't ready to talk about it. It probably had to do with the Marine Corps, she suspected. The Corps had a way of moving people a lot. Sometimes the moves were even classified! Fortunately, her own father was most likely going to stay right where he was for the rest of his career.

Colonel Hanson smiled at his friends. "You know, Jeanne used to tell me that instead of buying a house near whatever base I was stationed, we should just buy a moving van. It would save time packing the next time the Corps got another bright idea about my career!"

"You got that right!" Mrs. Devine joked. "Now, let's not talk about houses and moving anymore. It's too nice being here with old friends—and new ones," she said, smiling warmly at Carole. "So let's dig into the feast."

Carole quickly discovered that Colonel Devine was a fine barbecue chef, and Mrs. Devine's salads, munchies, and cool drinks made a great meal. They all enjoyed the fruit salad Carole had made, too.

After the two families had eaten more than their fill, everyone tidied up and packed the leftovers into the car. The colonels had challenged each other to a game of tennis, and Mrs. Devine had some errands to run. The girls were on their own.

"Great!" Carole said to Kate. "While our dads are at the courts, I can show you around the stables. I haven't been there for a long time, and I want to see some of my old friends. Drop us off there, will you, Dad? When we're done, we'll hitch a ride on a bus and meet you at the courts."

"When it comes to horses, dear daughter, you're never 'done.' We'll pick you up at the stables."

Carole just grinned as she swatted her father on the arm.

"I USED TO ride here almost every day," Carole told Kate as they approached the Quantico stables. "But when we moved to Willow Creek, it was too far, and, besides, I wanted to study with Max Regnery. He's a wonderful instructor. His former students include some Olympic riders. Can you *imagine?* It would be the most exciting thing in the world to be that good, I think."

"Hmm," Kate responded noncommittally.

"Well, I love the idea of that kind of competitive riding," Carole said. "It's like there would be a total focus on the most important part of my life—horses." She smiled, just thinking about the possibility, but when she glanced at Kate, she saw only confusion and doubt in her new friend's face. Carole guessed that Kate just wasn't turned on to horses—yet. "Come on, let's meet my friends," Carole invited, stepping into the stable. She was convinced that she could, and *would* change Kate's feeling about riding.

Kate followed her into the large structure where the base's horses were kept. Carole signed in with the stable manager, and explained that they were just visiting. Then she began the grand tour of the place.

Carole loved to share her information about horses, and felt she had a great opportunity to introduce Kate to the subject. Even her best friends, Stevie and Lisa, sometimes complained about how much she could talk about horses, but Kate just listened politely to Carole. Kate patted some of the horses and, Carole was pleased to observe, didn't seem in the least bit frightened of them. She had an easy and comfortable manner with the animals that wasn't matched by her words. Carole figured she had her work cut out for her.

"You'll be a good rider," Carole told Kate. "I can just see it in the way you handle the horses. You're not afraid of them. That's important."

"No, I'm not afraid, but, well, I—uh—" Kate seemed hesitant. "But I can't agree with you that I'll be a good rider."

"You'll see," Carole said confidently. "Come on, now, let me introduce you to another one of the horses I used to ride here. Now, this lady—she's called Duster because of the way she flicks her tail all the time—would do just fine on the trail, but she *hates* to be ridden indoors. She'll fuss and fume until she gets outside. . . ." Carole was off and running again, telling Kate more horse stories.

A half an hour later, Carole heard the familiar honk of her father's car horn. She and Kate signed back out of the stables and climbed in.

"Who won the tennis match?" Kate asked Colonel Hanson as she shut the car door.

"We've sworn each other to secrecy on the subject," Carole's father said mysteriously, shifting the car into gear. He pulled out onto the main road.

"That bad, huh?" Kate teased.

"I don't think I'll answer that one," the colonel said, but his grin gave him away. He turned the car toward Liversedge Hall.

"I think we have our answer," Kate told Carole.

"Did you girls enjoy the stables?" he asked, changing the subject smoothly.

"Oh, you know I always do," Carole answered. "But I'm afraid I ran on a bit about my favorite subject. I loaded poor Kate with one zillion details about horses. I didn't bore you, did I?"

"Oh, no," Kate told her. "It was interesting."

"And I guess you gave Carole a zillion details in return, didn't you, Kate?" Colonel Hanson asked. "I just knew you girls would hit it off. It's a good thing, too, because the Devines are going to come stay with us next weekend, Carole. We'll give them a taste of 'off-base housing,' to tempt them."

"Oh, great!" Carole said. "Then I can show you

Pine Hollow, too—and you can meet Stevie and Lisa. I've told you about them, right?"

"Yes, you did," Kate assured her. "I almost feel as if I know them already."

"Here you go, Kate," Colonel Hanson said, pulling up in front of Liversedge Hall. "We'll see you next weekend, okay?"

"Yes, thanks. And thanks for the lift, too," Kate said, stepping out of the car. "I'll see you next weekend, Carole." She stood back from the car and waved. Carole waved, too, until she couldn't see Kate anymore.

"She was really great, Dad. For once, you were absolutely right that I was going to like a friend's daughter."

"Well, you get along with most people so I knew it would be okay, but when the Devines told me about her riding, I knew you'd make a pair."

"What riding?" Carole asked.

"Kate's riding," he said.

"She didn't say anything to me about having ridden herself."

"That's odd," Colonel Hanson said. "Both Frank and Phyllis told me she was a really good rider. I thought they were just boasting. But it turns out Kate's a championship rider. She's gotten all kinds of blue ribbons and points in competitions. I can't believe she didn't tell you about it."

"Oh, no," Carole groaned, suddenly getting a really bad feeling in the pit of her stomach.

"What's the matter?" Colonel Hanson asked.

"I can't believe I did that!"

"What?" he asked.

"And I know who she is," Carole said.

"Of course you do. She's Frank and Phyllis's daughter."

"No, I don't mean that, Dad. I mean I've actually *read* about her. There was an article about her and how good she is and everything like that in a riding magazine. But they called her Katharine Devine, not Kate, so I didn't realize it was the same person—but it just has to be. Oh, I don't believe this!"

"What is the matter?"

"Dad, I just spent about an hour and a half lecturing her about basic horse stuff."

"What's wrong with that?" Colonel Hanson asked.

"Everything," Carole said. "It's like you telling the commandant of the Marine Corps that he should start with his left foot to march!" Carole shook her head in embarrassment and disbelief.

"I think I'm beginning to get the picture," her father said. "But there's no reason for you to feel bad, honey. After all, Kate had plenty of opportunities to tell you that she knew the things you were telling her. Why do you suppose she didn't?"

"Maybe because I was making a fool of myself?"

"She didn't strike me as the kind of person who enjoys making other people uncomfortable."

"Me neither," Carole said, shaking her head. "But

I—oh, no. I just get the shivers thinking about what I did." She shuddered.

"Relax, honey. It's not the end of the world. And you'll have a chance next weekend to figure it all out. Maybe you'll get her to lecture *you* for an hour and a half about horses, and—"

"Yeah, I guess," she interrupted her father. "At least I can have a lot of fun telling Stevie and Lisa about Kate. She's *famous*, Dad. Really."

" 'Famous' is relative, hon," he said to her. "And the only part about it that matters is how it affects people. It doesn't seem to me that it's affected Kate much."

"Maybe," Carole said. She recalled the quiet, almost withdrawn, girl who had followed her around the stable, listening politely. She compared her to the bright, funny, friendly girl she'd been talking with while they looked out over the water before lunch, or picnicked with their parents. Which one was *really* Kate Devine?

Carole was quiet for the rest of the trip home. She thought about Kate. The only thing she knew for sure was that her father was wrong. Somehow, something about riding *had* affected her. Carole decided to learn more when the Devines came to visit next weekend.

But in the meantime, she couldn't wait to tell Stevie and Lisa about Kate—and about her embarrassing mistake.

3

"I DON'T BELIEVE this," Stevie said, grimacing at her mother. They were sitting at the dinner table Saturday night. The Lakes always had a family dinner on Saturdays. It was the one night of the week when everybody was expected to be there. Sometimes the dinners were fun—like when they were planning family outings, or when Mr. and Mrs. Lake would talk about their own childhoods. At other times, like this one, the family dinners were gruesome.

Stevie's brother Chad had just delivered a bombshell. He had just announced that he intended to take up horseback riding—at Pine Hollow. Worse, he was going to start in the beginner class of the summer-camp program on Monday, which was just two days

20

away. Stevie looked to her mother for support, but Mrs. Lake was beaming at Chad.

"Mom!" Stevie said. "You can't let him do this!"

"Why, dear? What's wrong with Chad learning to ride horses?"

"Mom, he doesn't know the first thing about horses!"

"Neither did you when you started," Mrs. Lake reasoned.

"And he's just going to get in my hair," Stevie continued.

"How can he get in your hair if he's in a different class?"

"Yeah, bean brain," Chad chimed in.

"The place isn't all that big," Stevie said, ignoring him. "Besides, most of the beginners are like eight and nine years old. I'm sure he won't be wanting to spend much time with them. And if I know him, he's going to expect me to do his chores—"

"Chores?" Chad said. "What chores?" Stevie could tell by the surprise in his voice that he had no idea how much work it was to take care of horses. She might, just might, be able to talk him out of this scheme. At least she could hope.

"The chores *everybody* has to do, like, oh, mucking out stables, cleaning tack, and grooming the horses, which includes things like picking stones out of their hooves." She glanced at him sideways to judge his reaction. His face told her nothing. "You'd be amazed at the junk you can find in a horse's hoof," she added mysteriously.

"No problem," Chad said. "And besides, when you won't help me, I bet your friends, like Lisa, will."

Stevie tried another tack. "And sometimes, you have to give a horse medicine, like pouring milk of magnesia down his throat and holding his tongue at the same time."

"Oh, gross!" Stevie's twin, Alex, piped up, giving her hope.

"We are at the dinner table," Mrs. Lake observed mildly.

"Yeah, neat," Chad said, ignoring his mother, his eyes wide with excitement. "Did you ever do that?"

"No, I never did that," Stevie snapped back. She was irritated that he thought medicating a horse sounded like fun. Although she *was* prepared to do such a thing in an emergency, she dearly hoped that emergency would never arise.

"Stevie," her father spoke sternly. "Can we leave the subject now?"

"Yes, dear. Why don't you look on the bright side of things?" Mrs. Lake asked. "Think how nice it will be to have company while you're doing your chores."

"I usually have the company of my *friends*," she said. "I don't need a brother!"

"Stephanie, that is enough," her father said sternly.

Stevie hated to be called Stephanie and she knew

that her father knew that, too, so when her father called her Stephanie, he meant business. Reluctantly, she stopped talking, but they couldn't stop her from thinking how horrible it would be having Chad at Pine Hollow. She curled her lip in distaste.

As soon as she was finished, Stevie excused herself from the dinner table and went to her room. The one consolation of having three brothers and no sisters was that she had her own room. She could be alone.

As one of four children, Stevie often found herself involuntarily grouped with her brothers. Most of the time she didn't mind that. In fact, she usually enjoyed herself when they all got into something like a touch football game, or Frisbee, or when the family went to a movie that was an adventure more suitable for boys than girls. She was even proud of her tomboyishness, and, though she wasn't about to tell them, sometimes she was even proud of her brothers. But she was also proud of herself and the things she did by herself.

Riding was Number One.

When she thought about it, she realized that she didn't want Chad at Pine Hollow because it was *hers*. He didn't belong there. She didn't want to share Pine Hollow with her brothers—even just one of them. Riding was an experience she wanted to keep to herself.

But if her parents insisted that Chad be allowed to learn to ride, she had only one recourse. She would completely, absolutely, one hundred percent ignore him.

She reached for the phone, eager for the comfort of Carole's voice.

But something else was on Carole's mind.

"Katharine Devine! You mean the girl you showed us that article about? But she's famous, Carole—really famous. I mean, she's one of the best junior riders in the country. And she's coming to your house next weekend!" Stevie said in awe.

"Isn't that something?" Carole said. "I feel so lucky just to know her, and wait until you meet her—"

"Can I?" Stevie asked.

"Of course you can," Carole said. "In fact, I'm thinking of asking Dad if you and Lisa can sleep over on Friday night. Kate is coming on Saturday morning, so you'd both be here."

"Kate?" Stevie echoed. "It sounds like you're so friendly already!"

"Well, she's really just a person like you or me. Actually, she's a little older, I guess fourteen or fifteen, but she's so *nice*—and so normal. At least I think she is."

"You're not sure she's normal?" Stevie asked.

Carole explained that she and Kate had spent a couple of hours together, a lot of the time with Carole talking about horses, and Kate had never even mentioned that she rode, much less that she was a champion.

"Maybe she just didn't want to embarrass you," Stevie said.

"You're probably right," Carole agreed. "But the fact is that I *am* embarrassed. Can you imagine *me* telling Kate Devine about how important it is to let horses cool down after a ride?"

"I can imagine you telling anybody anything about horses," Stevie joked. "After all, if Lisa and I let you get started—"

"Enough, enough," Carole said, laughing. "I plead guilty."

"That's okay, Carole," Stevie assured her. "We still love you. And besides, whenever there's something we actually *don't* know, you come in awfully handy."

"Thanks. So, what about Friday night?"

"I wouldn't miss it for anything. My mother will say yes, I'm pretty sure. After all, she owes me."

"She owes you?" Carole asked. "What does that mean?"

"That's the bad news," Stevie began mournfully. "All of a sudden, my brother Chad has decided that he wants to learn to ride. So, Mom has signed him up for the beginner camp program for the month. Can you believe it? Dumb old Chad is going to be at Pine Hollow every single day."

"I know he's your brother and all, Stevie," Carole said, "but he's not really all that bad. Remember the time we were having a Saddle Club meeting at your house and he brought us cookies and milk?"

"Okay, so once in his total fourteen years, he wasn't a doofus," Stevie conceded graciously.

25

Carole could barely stifle her giggles. "Give him a chance, will you?"

"One," Stevie agreed. "But the first time he makes a fool of himself, I'm going to disown him." She paused for a second. "No, I can't do that," she said. "That means I'd be cutting him out of my will, and I've already done that. I cut him out when he told Will Chambers that I'd written his name one hundred times in my social studies book."

"Did you?" Carole asked.

"Sure I did," Stevie told her. "But I didn't want Will to know it."

"I think I'm beginning to see how a brother could be a drawback," Carole said, laughing. "Don't worry, though. Lisa and I will protect you from him."

"Thanks," Stevie told Carole. "Hey, I think I hear my mother coming upstairs. I'm going to ask her now about the sleepover on Friday. I'll let you know Monday. I'm sure the answer will be yes, though. Bye-bye," she said hurriedly. She hung up the phone and bounced up off her bed. She had to find her mother right away, while her mother still felt guilty.

CAROLE STARED AT the phone in her hand, smiling in bewilderment. She hadn't even had a chance to say good-bye to Stevie before Stevie had hung up. What a girl her friend was! Stevie bounced from misery to joy faster than anybody Carole had ever known—and from joy back to misery just as fast! Having Chad at the stable couldn't possibly be as bad as Stevie said it would be, Carole thought. There weren't that many boys there, either, so it might even be nice to have him around. How bad could it be? Carole asked herself. Shrugging, she decided to check with her father about the sleepover on Friday and then call Lisa. Then, after that, she'd make a list of the questions she wanted to ask Kate about riding in general, and about being a champion, in particular.

Kate Devine. Katharine Devine. Carole repeated the name to herself. She could barely believe that she was actually going to come to her house, maybe even be her friend. Kate might even ride at Pine Hollow!

ON MONDAY MORNING, Lisa was in the locker area of the stables when Stevie stormed in, mumbling to herself.

"What's up?" Lisa asked innocently, though she was sure she already knew what Stevie was steaming about.

"In about three minutes, Max is going to call me over the P.A. and ask me to help Chad get acquainted with the stable. I'm going to have to show my stupid brother how to tack up a horse."

"Take it easy, Stevie," Lisa said, trying to calm her. Sometimes she could joke Stevie out of being angry, but this wasn't one of them. Stevie was in no mood to see the humor of the situation. Only time could cure this. "Look, if it'll help, I'll come along too. Then I can help you help him." Lisa grinned at her mixed-up-sounding sentence, but Stevie didn't seem to notice.

Stevie reached for her jodhpur boots and pulled them on. "Where's Carole?" she asked.

"She's in the paddock with Delilah and Samson," Lisa explained. Samson was a two-week-old colt, Delilah's son. The Saddle Club had been alone at the stable with Delilah when Samson had been born, and now the three girls watched over the black colt like doting aunts. Carole, especially, liked to spend time with the spindle-legged colt. "I was in the paddock, too, before you got here. Delilah was swishing at flies with her tail, and Samson was cuddled up next to her."

That made Stevie grin. "He's *so* cute," she said.

"Who, *me?*" a voice asked from the door to the locker area.

Lisa turned to see Chad, standing next to Max. Stevie glared at Chad. "No, not you, Chad. You're definitely *not* cute. We were talking about a colt."

Max seemed unaware of the icy exchange, but Lisa suspected he was actually just ignoring it. He cleared his throat. The students looked at him. "Stevie, I'd like you to show Chad around the stable and then I'd like you to show him how to put the tack on Patch. His class begins in half an hour. Until then, you're excused from chores. See you in class, Chad."

Max left the locker area, leaving Chad to the mercies of Lisa and Stevie. Chad didn't seem in the least upset. Stevie did. Lisa decided to try to break the ice a bit.

"I knew you were wrong about Max," she said to Stevie.

Stevie stared at her in surprise.

"Well"—Lisa shrugged—"you said he'd call you over the P.A. He actually came here in person."

Stevie gave her the tiniest bit of a grin.

Lisa tried to finish her chores quickly so she could join Stevie and Chad. She had the feeling war would be declared between the two of them if they were left alone for long. It had surprised her a little that Max had asked Stevie to show Chad around. Usually Max showed better judgment than that. He must have known that Stevie wouldn't like it—unless, of course, Chad had asked Max to get Stevie to give him the tour. But why would he have done that?

Lisa brought the last bucket of fresh water to the ponies, latched it onto the hook on the wall, and went in search of the Lakes. It wasn't hard to find them. All she had to do was to follow the sound of the sarcastic voice.

"Okay, Chad," Stevie said through gritted teeth. "This is Patch." She held the horse, a gentle pinto that Max usually used for beginners, by his halter. Lisa walked over to Patch's stall and stood on her tiptoes to see over the door. She greeted Stevie and Chad. Stevie was preoccupied and barely acknowledged her, but Chad greeted her with a warm smile.

"Do you know the first thing about tacking up?" Stevie asked.

"Sure!" Chad said. "You got to put the pedal to the metal," he replied.

"What are you talking about?"

"You know, like 'tach it up'—like with a car?" He seemed surprised by Stevie's and Lisa's blank looks. "The tachometer—it measures the RPM of the crankshaft. You do know what that is, don't you?"

"No, I don't," Stevie said. "And I don't think Patch has one, anyway."

Chad looked to Lisa for support, but she was as confused as Stevie. Chad shrugged.

"Lesson number one," Stevie said to Chad. "This is the front end." She pointed to Patch's nose. "And this isn't." She pointed toward his tail.

"You don't have to be sarcastic," Chad said.

"Max told me I had to show you around and help you tack up. He didn't say I had to be nice to you, did he?"

"No, I guess not," Chad agreed. "But it'll go better for both of us if you are."

She gave him a withering look and then sighed. "Okay. First, the saddle." She showed him how to smooth the saddle pad on the horse's back and how to put the saddle on over it, gently, so as not to startle the mount.

As she finished fastening the girth, showing Chad how to test it for tightness and how to pull at the

31

buckle gently instead of yanking it, Lisa came into the stall to help tighten the girth.

"You know Lisa, right?" Stevie asked by way of introduction.

"Yeah, uh—sure, I do," Chad said. "We've met a *lot* of times, Lisa, haven't we?" He seemed almost eager to make the point.

"Hi, Chad," Lisa responded. "You're going to get a lot of information today. Good luck."

"Oh, thanks," he said. "I'm really looking forward to it, too. You're a pretty new rider, aren't you?" he asked.

"Yes," Lisa told him. "I've just been riding since last spring—"

"Are you in the beginner class, too?" he asked.

"Nope," Lisa said. "Max put me in with the older kids. He'll probably graduate you at the end of the summer. Most of the riders in the beginner class are, well, pretty young."

"Really? I thought Stevie just said that to discourage me. But as long as I'll move up quickly."

"About a month," Lisa told him.

"If it's all right with you two, I'll show Chad how to put on a bridle," Stevie interrupted.

"I bet I'll really bridle at that," Chad joked.

"Huh?" Stevie grunted. Lisa giggled.

"*Bridle* at that," Chad repeated. "You know, bridle, like resent something? It's a joke," he explained to Stevie.

"Not a very good one," Stevie said, but Lisa didn't think he'd heard his sister. Chad was just looking at her and grinning. It embarrassed Lisa. She could feel herself flush red. She hoped neither Stevie nor Chad would notice. If they did, they didn't say anything.

"And you slide the crownpiece over the horse's ears, smoothing down the mane. Be sure his forelock isn't stuck in the browband. Then you fasten the throatlatch and—Chad, what are you *doing?*" Stevie stopped abruptly, realizing she still didn't have his attention.

"There's a cat in here!" he said.

"There are cats all over here," Stevie told him. "All stables are full of cats. They keep the mouse population down. Now, here's how you fasten—"

"Here, kitty, kitty," he said.

"Grrr," Stevie said.

"Is there a dog around here, too?" Chad asked.

"This is going to get rough," Stevie warned, gritting her teeth.

"I *thought* I heard a dog."

"I give up," Stevie said. She slid under the horse's neck and walked over to the door. "Lisa, can you take over for me? I know he's hopeless, but he may be less hopeless with you than he is with me. I wouldn't usually do this to a *friend.* In fact, if my worst enemy were handy . . ."

"Don't worry, Stevie," Lisa assured her. "I'll cope. It's fifteen minutes to our trail class. I'll get Chad to the ring. Can you bring Pepper's tack to his stall for me?"

"Gladly," Stevie said, escaping from Patch's enclosure. Lisa and Chad could hear her sighing with relief as she headed for the tack room.

Chad listened intently while Lisa explained the rest of the tacking procedure. However, when he asked which was the bridle and which was the halter, Lisa got the distinct impression that he wasn't taking in much of the information. *What is he up to?* she asked herself.

Within a few minutes, Patch was ready for class, though Lisa wasn't sure about Chad. She showed him how to lead the horse to the ring.

"Don't look at him," she said. "Just look straight ahead and walk forward, tugging gently on the reins. See, if you stare at him, he'll stare back at you, and the two of you will just be standing there, staring at each other."

Chad looked over his shoulder into the horse's eyes. The horse stared back at him. Finally, he turned and faced forward, and began walking. "I see what you mean," he said sheepishly.

Lisa brought him to the indoor ring and showed him the well-worn good-luck horseshoe. "You just have to touch it before you mount," she explained. "It's one of our traditions. See, as long as this has been here and the riders have been touching it before mounting, no rider has gotten badly hurt."

"What about the horses?" Chad joked, nevertheless giving the horseshoe a brief touch.

"Horses *do* get hurt sometimes, mostly by careless riders. Maybe we ought to put out a riding boot the horses can paw at before letting anyone mount them," she said, laughing.

Lisa then took a few minutes to show Chad how to mount properly. When Chad was on Patch, she wished him good luck quickly, then hustled away to tack up Pepper for her own class.

As she readied Pepper, she thought about Chad. She had met him several times before at Stevie's house, and he had always seemed nice enough, but he'd never shown any interest at all in riding. What was behind this big change? Lisa wondered.

Stevie always said the only thing Chad was interested in was girls. Well, there were certainly a lot of girls around Pine Hollow. Could it be—Lisa suddenly got a funny feeling. She remembered how Chad had grinned when he'd seen her, and how he'd been so eager to learn from her, as opposed to the way he'd teased Stevie. And she remembered a time she'd been to Stevie's house when Stevie wasn't there. Chad had tried to get her to stay and hang out, even though Stevie wasn't around. Lisa's funny feeling was turning into a hunch, and the hunch was that Chad had a crush—on *her*!

If she was right, she could be in hot water with Stevie. But that wouldn't be fair. She hadn't done anything to encourage Chad. She hadn't been flirting with him. And besides, even if he did have some kind of crush on her, it didn't mean he had to ride horses! Suddenly things were looking very complicated.

Lisa decided to think about this some more. She had gotten to the point of trying to figure out if she liked Chad or not when she was interrupted.

"Did you deliver my brother to the ring on time?" Stevie asked.

"As advertised," Lisa said. "Once you'd gone, he paid more attention and stopped making so many jokes. You shouldn't take it all so seriously, you know. He's not all that bad."

"He's not your brother," Stevie said darkly. But Lisa thought maybe things would be simpler for her if he *were* her brother, instead of a boy with a crush on her. Maybe.

Just then, Carole passed by, leading Diablo. "Red is ready to go now. Are you finished?" she asked Lisa. Red O'Malley was the instructor on their trail ride that morning.

Lisa nodded and brought Pepper out of his stall to follow Diablo toward the door. One thing she was sure of about Chad was that if she kept her suspicions to herself, Stevie would figure out she was hiding something. They just had to talk. Carole would be a help, too.

"Hey, guys?" Lisa said to her friends, speaking loudly to be heard over the clump of hooves on the wooden floor of the stable. "How about a Saddle Club meeting this afternoon at TD's?" Tastee Delight was the ice cream store at the nearby shopping center, and their favorite meeting place.

"Hungry already?" Carole joked.

"Not yet," Lisa said, suspecting she wouldn't have much of an appetite when she had to tell Stevie about Chad. "But I probably will be by then."

"Great idea," Stevie said. "Chad's sure to want a long, hot bath as soon as he leaves the stable—he's going to be sore today! It'll be a chance for some privacy. But—oh, no," she groaned as she felt her pockets.

"What's the matter?" Carole asked.

"I'm out of money," Stevie said. Carole and Lisa had to stifle giggles. The fact was that Stevie was *always* out of money.

"My treat today," Carole offered. "After all, we have to make plans for the weekend." She brought her horse outside and mounted him smoothly. Stevie followed suit.

Lisa was the third to mount. She held her reins and her riding whip in her left hand and slid her left foot into the stirrup. Red O'Malley gave her a boost. In a moment, she was in the saddle and her feet were in the stirrups. It was going to be a relief to concentrate on horses instead of boys for a while.

CAROLE NEEDED TIME to talk to Stevie alone. She maneuvered the afternoon chores so she and Stevie left the stable before Lisa did. Carole told Lisa they'd meet her at TD's. Lisa promised she'd be there about fifteen minutes later.

When they first got to TD's, Carole couldn't get a word in edgewise. She and Stevie sat at a booth in the back of the shop and, from practically the moment they arrived, Stevie just talked about her brother.

"Could you believe it?" Stevie asked. "At lunch, when he started doing that stupid cowboy imitation? What does he think this stable is? And then all the little kids were laughing—"

"It *was* funny," Carole reminded Stevie. "Even I laughed."

"Maybe. But why? What's he trying to do to me?"

"Stevie!" Carole said in exasperation. "What he's doing doesn't have anything to do with you."

"Of course it does," Stevie protested. "Why else would he be making a fool of himself? He's just trying to embarrass me. And the worst part is that he's succeeding."

"Stevie, think," Carole said.

"I can't think," Stevie said. "Every time I try to think, all I can think *of* is doofus. So what are you talking about?"

Carole took a spoonful of her sundae, hoping a pause in the conversation would help to calm Stevie a bit. When she'd finished swallowing, she spoke.

"Your brother is just doing what you say Chad *always* does," Carole said patiently and calmly. "He is trying to get a girl's attention."

"Okay—but why does he have to do that around *me?*" Stevie demanded.

"Because the girl in question is always around you," Carole said.

Stevie looked at Carole sideways. Carole could tell from the look on her face that Stevie was beginning to see the light. "Are you saying what I think you're saying?" Stevie asked after a pause.

"If you think I'm saying that Chad has a crush on Lisa, you're right. I don't think he's really into riding—he just wants to be where she is."

Stevie furrowed her brow and stared at her glass of water.

"Does Lisa know this?" Stevie asked finally.

"I'm not sure, but she'll figure it out soon enough," Carole said. "After all, Chad isn't exactly being subtle."

"I can't believe I didn't think of that myself!" Stevie said. "Of course, you're absolutely right. He's been talking about her, but I didn't think anything of it, since I talk about both of you all the time. Well, I'll just tell him Lisa hasn't got the slightest interest in the whole wide world in being his girlfriend and that's that. He can just get lost."

"Hold it," Carole said, raising her hand as if to stop traffic. "You can't do that. If Lisa wants to stop Chad, she can tell him herself. And if she doesn't want to stop him—well, then you shouldn't butt in."

"You mean one of my best friends may actually *want* to be my brother's girlfriend?" Stevie asked.

"I don't know," Carole said. "But I do think that you should let true love take its course," she added with a grin.

"Oh, groan," Stevie said.

"Don't worry about it. Lisa's pretty smart," Carole reminded her. "She'll know how to handle it."

"I'll keep that in mind. But the hardest thing to remind myself is going to be that I shouldn't just tell him to drop dead."

"Maybe Lisa will," Carole suggested.

"My brother? She'd say *that* to *my* brother?" Stevie asked, suddenly on the defensive.

"Let's change the subject, huh?" Carole suggested. "Here comes Lisa. And it looks like she's got something on her mind."

Lisa walked toward the booth slowly. She slid in next to Carole, almost without seeing her. Lisa pushed up her sleeves and leaned forward on the table until she was looking Stevie straight in the eye.

"There's something I have to tell you," Lisa said. "I think I've figured out the reason Chad suddenly wants to learn to ride," she began. She was about to continue when Stevie interrupted her.

"I know," she said lightly. "He's got a crush on you."

Lisa stared at her. "How'd you know?"

"It just sort of hit me," Stevie said, glancing at Carole. "Like a ton of bricks. Don't worry about it. It doesn't really *mean* anything, you know—" Carole gave her a quick, dirty look. "I mean, it doesn't mean anything to *me*."

"I feel pretty confused, you know."

"Who wouldn't?" Carole said. "But we'll have all night on Friday to talk, and maybe figure out what to do. For now, let's talk about something *really* important."

"What?" both Stevie and Lisa asked together.

"Kate Devine!"

-5-

WHEN STEVIE FINALLY stopped to think about it calmly, a few days after Chad had started at the stable, she realized that she was going to be too busy there to pay much attention to her brother—and that he was going to be well-occupied, too.

"You know," she said to Carole as they were sitting on the bench in the tack room, cleaning tack, "I'd forgotten how much the beginners have to learn." She tugged at the bridle she was cleaning. While she was trying to get accumulated dirt off the leather, one of the stable's kittens was chasing the throatlatch, which dangled invitingly from the bridle. Stevie swished it across the floor. The kitten pounced on it happily.

"There's a lot of information beginners have got to

master just to ride safely—even at a walk," Carole agreed.

"You sound like a professor when you talk that way," Stevie told her, grinning. "Actually, all I care about is for Max to keep Chad so busy he can't get in my hair."

"Room for one more?" Lisa asked, entering the tack room.

"You bet there is," Stevie said, welcoming her. "Mrs. Reg seems to think every piece of leather in the place is dirty. That's about forty saddles—not counting the special ones—and of course, *they* need cleaning, too."

"I'll get a fresh dish of water and a sponge for myself. Make room for me on the bench, will you?"

"Sure!" Carole said, scooting over. "Don't complain, though—I want to have all the tack clean by this weekend."

"What's so special about this weekend?" Stevie asked. "The three-day event and the gymkhana aren't for another couple of weeks—how many hours, Lisa?"

"Um, exactly—I don't remember," she confessed as she joined her friends on the bench. She sat down, picking up a bridle of her own. The kitten who had been chasing Stevie's bridle jumped up on the bench near Lisa. She patted its soft fur and then set the animal back down on the floor. The kitten then seemed confused about which bridle to attack. "Oh, they *are* cute, aren't they? If only I thought Dolly would put up with a kitten . . ." Lisa said, referring to her dog, a Lhasa apso. "But she's too set in her ways now. Anyway, we were talking about this weekend. What's the rush on cleaning tack?"

"Well, I'm going to bring Kate Devine here on Saturday," Carole explained.

"You think she'll be inspecting the tack?" Stevie asked, glancing at Carole.

Carole just glared at her. Stevie decided that meant that Carole *did* think Kate would care. Stevie found that hard to imagine.

"Speaking of Kate," Stevie began. "Meg Durham and Polly Giacomin were asking me about her this morning."

"Why didn't they ask *me*?" Carole said, surprised.

"They wanted to know who she was and how come she was so famous. Since you've been talking about her so much, they were embarrassed that they hadn't heard of her. Meg thought maybe Kate Devine was some kind of superstar—"

"Oh, but she *is*," Carole began. "Do you have any idea how difficult it is for anyone to become a championship rider? I mean, that's hours and hours of studying over years and years, including hard physical work, to say nothing of the horse care involved—and then the tension of the competition—and the thrill of victory . . ." Carole got a dreamy look on her face as her voice trailed off.

Stevie and Lisa exchanged glances, winking at each

other. Carole was like that. She was their friend and they were more than willing to accept her hang-ups. But that didn't mean they couldn't share a grin about them from time to time.

"You know, Carole, I've been thinking about the costume race in the gymkhana. Do you think you could get a Marine Corps uniform from your father? That would be neat, especially if it had a lot of buttons some *other* team had to do up."

"Oh, sure," Carole said, returning abruptly from her daydream. "He's got some junky old ones we can use. The only thing he'll insist on is that we remove the Marine Corps emblems before using it for games."

"Guess what I heard," Lisa said. "Max is going to make up the gymkhana teams next week. He's just *got* to let us be on a team together."

"It probably depends on having evenly matched teams," Carole reminded her.

"Well, I've had my fingers crossed," Stevie said. "But it makes it awfully difficult to ride that way!"

Carole and Lisa both burst into laughter at Stevie's joke. Their noise frightened the kitten into retreat.

"I hear more talk than tack cleaning going on in there," Mrs. Reg called from her office next to the tack room. She leaned across her desk so she could see the girls. Stevie could tell Mrs. Reg was trying to look stern. She wasn't very good at it.

Mrs. Reg was Max's mother. When her husband had died and her son had taken over management of the stable, she had continued being in charge of the stable's equipment, as she had done for half a century. She also sometimes served as substitute mother to the young riders when one was called for and she was always full of stories about horses and riders. The students at Pine Hollow claimed that Mrs. Reg had a story for every possible circumstance. She'd seen it all—or at least she *said* she had.

"Mrs. Reg," Stevie said. "Give us a break. We're working very hard. It's just that there's so much to talk about."

"I know, I know," she said, relenting and stepping into the tack room from her office. "We once had a rider here—oh, it was before you girls were born . . ."

Mrs. Reg had found the surest way to have the girls stop chitchatting among themselves—not that she really cared. Stevie suspected that sometimes Mrs. Reg would pretend to chide them about one thing or another when she actually just wanted an excuse to tell a story. It was okay as far as Stevie was concerned. Stevie reached forward to the tin of saddle soap and rubbed her sponge on the soap until she'd worked up a lather.

Mrs. Reg joined the girls on the bench and went on. "This woman, I've forgotten her name, was the kind that really kept to herself. She rode here often, and even took lessons from Max. My husband, Max, that is. Not *your* Max, as you sometimes call him. Anyway, this woman rode here and did chores here, just the same way you girls do, but she never said anything to anybody. Never made friends at all. Too bad." Mrs. Reg stopped talking. The girls were surprised because she sounded as if she were finished with her story, but it didn't seem to be an ending.

"What do you mean by 'too bad'?" Carole asked after a few seconds.

"I mean it was too bad she never talked to anybody," Mrs. Reg said, as if that were an explanation.

"So, *what* happened?" Stevie asked.

Mrs. Reg looked at the girls' faces and apparently realized that the ending wasn't clear. "What happened is that she stopped riding. See, she didn't have any friends. Riding is a friendly sport and if you never talk with anybody about it, you're missing half the fun."

"Boy, can I understand that," Stevie said. "Does that mean we should talk with one another whenever we want to?"

"It does not," Mrs. Reg announced. "Now, finish up. Max told me you three were going to talk to the beginner class about the gymkhana. I'm sure they're almost ready for you now."

"Yes'm," Carole said. Mrs. Reg returned to her desk, and the girls put the cleaning gear back on the shelves.

"Mrs. Reg is something, isn't she?" Lisa asked as they walked toward the beginner class.

"She sure is," Stevie said. "But sometimes I wish it were clearer exactly what she was saying."

"You understood that story, didn't you?" Carole asked Lisa.

"Easy!" Lisa chimed in. "I think she was saying it was okay to talk, even if the rule says we aren't supposed to, because being friends is important. So it must be your favorite kind of rule, Stevie. It's the kind you're supposed to break!"

Stevie laughed. Her friends knew her well. She felt very sorry for that woman who had given up riding because she didn't have friends. She had missed out on two of the best things in the world.

6

"ARE YOU SURE you know what you're doing?" Lisa asked.

"Absolutely," Stevie responded with total confidence. "I've done this lots." She combed some styling mousse into Lisa's damp hair. Then she separated a small section, held it straight up, and rolled it onto a curler. "See, the first thing you have to do is to give the hair some body—curl, I mean—then you can style it anyway you want."

Lisa's eyes met Stevie's in the mirror. They were filled with doubt.

"Trust me," Stevie said reassuringly.

"Those are the very words the executioner said to Marie Antoinette," Carole teased. She was watching the entire procedure from a safe distance away, on her bed. It was Friday night and The Saddle Club girls were enjoying their sleepover at Carole's house. Carole was observing her friend's makeover, but her mind kept jumping to Kate Devine's much-anticipated visit the next day.

"Some help *you* are," Stevie complained. "Here Lisa is, nervous as a cat about her new look, and you try to tell her I'm an executioner? Thanks."

"Well, let's face it," Carole said. "Marie Antoinette's new hairdo was permanent—"

"Yuck, what a thought!" Lisa squirmed in her seat.

"I'm just joking," Carole said.

"Yeah? Well, if you were sitting where I am, you wouldn't think it was so funny."

"No, I guess not! I'm sorry. I was actually thinking about Kate."

"Well, that's okay," Stevie said. "I've been thinking about her, too. Do you think she'd let me try a new style on *her* hair?"

Carole grinned, imagining Stevie doing Kate's hair. "I don't know. You could ask her. Oh, guess what—the original *King Kong* is on TV tonight. I asked Dad if we could watch it and he said okay."

"It's only from eight to ten," Stevie said. "How come you had to ask his permission?"

"It wasn't getting his permission to watch it," Carole explained. "It was getting his okay to watch it without him. See, it's one of his favorite movies."

"Your dad's a pretty neat guy," Stevie said. "And I'm

sure he knows better than to try to join in on our pajama party. That's much better than at *my* house where we'd be fighting off three boys." As she finished speaking, she fastened the final curler with a clip, folded her hands neatly in front of her, and bowed politely, waiting for applause.

Carole clapped. Lisa was about to and then thought better of it. "I think I'll wait until I see the final result," she teased.

"If it's really weird, will you show it to your mother?" Stevie asked, turning a blow-dryer on and aiming it at the curlers.

"If it's really weird, I'll wash it out," Lisa said.

"Ah, Lisa the A student," Stevie joked. "Always has a solution to every problem. Is that why you wouldn't let me do the frosting?"

"Well, that's one of the reasons," Lisa said evasively.

"You have no faith in me," Stevie said in mock hurt.

"That's one way to put it," Lisa joked. Then she glanced at her watch. "Come on, hurry up, it's almost eight o'clock. Time for *King Kong*. ''Twas *beauty* killed the beast,'" she quoted, her voice suddenly deep and ominous.

"Boy, I love that movie," Carole said.

"Me, too," Stevie agreed. "Do we have time to make popcorn?"

"There's always time for popcorn," Carole assured her, heading for the kitchen. "You go and turn on the TV. I'll be there in a minute."

• • •

"OH, THAT POOR monster," Carole wailed two hours later, wiping tears from her cheeks. "Can you imagine? Why couldn't they just leave him alone? How can people be so cruel to animals? Weren't there any animal-rights people around?" she demanded.

"It really is awful what people can do sometimes, isn't it?" Lisa joined in while she and Carole tidied up the kitchen, putting their bowls and glasses in the dishwasher.

"You guys!" Stevie chimed in from the den, where she was replacing the pillows and picking up stray pieces of popcorn. "It's only a movie!"

"I know it's only a movie," Carole said, calming down. "But it reminds me how people sometimes just use animals without remembering that they have minds and feelings, too."

"Maybe when you grow up, instead of owning a horse farm, you'll be an animal-rights activist," Lisa suggested.

"Maybe I'll be an animal-rights activist in *addition* to owning a horse farm," Carole countered, leading Lisa to the stairs.

"And in addition to being a vet? And a trainer?" Stevie asked, meeting them at the landing.

"I don't think I'm ready to make up my mind," Carole said. "I just know I want to be with horses. That's as far as I've gotten. What about you guys? You going to be a beautician?" she asked Stevie with a grin.

"We'll see about that," Lisa said, patting the curlers to see if her hair was dry. It was. "Do your thing!" she said to Stevie.

Carole hauled the sleeping bags out of the closet and arranged them on the floor while Stevie prepared to comb out Lisa's light brown hair. When the sleeping bags were laid out, Carole perched on the edge of her bed to watch the unveiling. Carefully, Stevie unrolled each curler, figuring Lisa's hair would wave gently to her shoulders, but that wasn't what happened at all. As each curler was removed, the hair bounced right back into a tight curl, as if the curler were still there.

"Is this okay?" Lisa asked dubiously.

"Oh, sure," Stevie said, but the look on her face showed concern. When the final curler was removed, she took Lisa's hairbrush and began smoothing out the curls. Each time she brushed through Lisa's hair, the curls rewound into their coils.

"I'm getting a bad feeling about this," Lisa said. "This isn't what you had in mind, was it?"

Stevie was doing everything she could to keep a straight face, brushing more and more vigorously at the tight curls, but when it became clear that it wasn't going to work—that Lisa's hair was determined to stay tightly coiled—she could contain it no longer. She simply exploded into giggles.

For a second, Carole was afraid Lisa was going to be angry with Stevie, but looking at herself in the mirror, Lisa quickly joined Stevie. While she laughed, she bounced her head up and down, watching each curl behave like a Slinky.

"It's just not me," she said between giggles.

"It's certainly *different*," Carole said, joining in the laughter. "Maybe if you sleep on it—" she suggested.

"I think I'll wet it down first," Lisa said. "And, the whole time I'm wetting it down, I'm going to be thankful I *didn't* let you frost it!"

"Me, too," Stevie said, giggles subsiding. "Want me to help you wet it?"

Lisa gave her a sidelong glance. "No thanks!" she said airily, heading for the bathroom. That got Carole and Stevie laughing again.

By the time Lisa returned, wet-headed and straight-haired, Carole and Stevie were climbing into their sleeping bags. Lisa retreated to hers, a dry towel on the pillow to protect it from the dampness of her hair. Carole turned out the light and the girls settled in for some serious talking.

"I just can't wait to see Kate again," Carole began.

"She must be neat," Stevie said.

"Oh, yes, she is! And she's *different*, somehow, too."

"Different from whom?" Lisa asked.

"Everybody," Carole said. "She seems so sure of herself, so confident. But it's not off-putting, if you know what I mean."

"I guess you have to be pretty sure of yourself if

you're going to be in tough competitions like she has," Lisa observed.

"I guess you do," Carole said. "But she's not snooty, like you might think she could be."

"We'll see for ourselves soon enough," Stevie said.

"Just about twelve hours from now," Lisa piped in.

"I can't wait," Carole said again.

"So we heard," Lisa said.

"Have I been talking about her too much?" Carole asked. Lisa could hear the hurt in Carole's voice and was ashamed of herself for her thoughtless remark.

"Oh, I didn't mean it that way," she said, trying to comfort Carole. "I was just teasing. But—"

"But what?" Carole asked.

"Sometimes you do go on a bit," Lisa said. "But it's okay. It's you and that's the way you are—like how you sometimes lecture a bit on horse care. That's okay, too, because your friends really learn from you, you know? So now you're excited about Kate—"

"Sure I'm excited about her arriving, but maybe I'm talking about it so much because, in a way, I'm dreading it, too."

"You could fool me!" Stevie said. "Why are you nervous?"

"Well, it's that thing about how I kept sort of giving her that beginner lesson in horses last week—and then I learn that she's an expert! What do you suppose she thinks of me? I made such an idiot of myself!"

"You're not an idiot," Lisa assured her. "And besides, the big question here is, *why* didn't she tell you? It's not as if she could have just expected you to know about her blue ribbons—"

"Not just blue ribbons," Carole interrupted. "She's got to have a roomful of silver cups!"

"But she couldn't expect you to know about them. So *why?*"

"I don't know why, but I do know *what*. The what is that as soon as I see her tomorrow, I have to apologize."

"I bet she apologizes first," Stevie said.

"What does she have to apologize for?" Carole asked. "She didn't make a fool out of herself."

"No, but she made you feel embarrassed, and that's worse," Lisa said. "If she's as nice as you say, there's got to be a reason. The big mystery for tomorrow is going to be finding it out."

"Maybe," Carole said.

Lisa could tell, though, that she still felt bad about the whole mix-up. But they couldn't solve the mystery until Kate arrived. In the meantime, Lisa had to get Carole's mind off it. "Time to change the subject," she announced. "Anybody have something else to talk about?"

"I do," Stevie said. "I want to talk about B-O-Y-S."

"Yes?" Carole said, obviously relieved to have the focus off herself. "Anyone in particular?"

"Sort of," Stevie said. "I was wondering what it's like

to have a boy have a crush on you. I don't think that's ever happened to me," she said. "I thought maybe Lisa . . . ?"

Lisa was quiet for a moment. She hadn't been terribly comfortable this week, being sure Chad was sort of lurking around, thinking about her. She *wanted* to talk about it, but, after all, Stevie was his sister. She took a deep breath. Lisa didn't think she'd ever be able to talk about Chad, or any other boy, in the daylight. But, somehow, when the lights were out and they couldn't see one another's faces, it was easier to share.

"It's kind of strange, to tell you the truth. I mean, it's like—well, he must know that I know he has a crush on me, but still nothing has happened."

"Do you want something to happen?" Carole asked.

"Oh, yes!" Lisa said. "I've never had a date. I can hardly wait for my first date. And he *is* kind of cute," Lisa added, glancing at Stevie. "But I'm scared at the same time, you know what I mean? And it's funny, knowing there are these feelings, like they're hanging around in the air, but everybody's pretending not to notice them."

"I saw a movie once where this boy and girl just looked at each other and they were madly in love and they never even had to say anything to each other because they each knew exactly what was on the other's mind. It was so romantic!" Carole said, almost breathlessly.

"Uckko!" Stevie said. "I sure don't want any boy to

know what's on my mind! It was awful when Will Chambers knew what I was thinking because *somebody* told him."

"But what if it were like your minds were one?" Carole persisted.

"I don't want any part of it if that means he'd know how badly I did on my last science test."

"That's not what we're talking about at all," Lisa said. "We're talking about *romance.*" She sighed dreamily.

"Maybe," Stevie said dubiously. "But somehow I can't picture the word 'romance' and my brother Chad in the same room. Can you, honestly, Lisa?"

"Oh, I don't know," Lisa said. "That's part of what's so confusing about this whole thing. But you should realize that he's not *my* brother and I just don't see him the same way you do. I don't think of him as the boy who uses the last of the soap, or borrows your hairbrush—"

"Or chews with his mouth open, or who teases me about all sorts of things. Okay, okay. So, then, how *do* you think of him?" Stevie asked.

"I guess lately I've been thinking of him as maybe the boy who might ask me out," she confessed in the darkness.

There was a long silence and then Carole spoke. "First date," she said, as if she were entranced by the mere sound of the words.

"It could be years away," Lisa reasoned.

"And it could be next week," Carole reminded her.

"And it could be with my *brother*!" Stevie said.

With those thoughts on their minds, the girls eventually drifted into sleep.

7

CAROLE GLANCED AT the clock for the umpteenth time Saturday morning. The Devines would arrive any minute now, she knew. She looked out the window again.

"They'll get here, honey," her father said. "Frank said they'd arrive between ten and eleven. It's only ten-fifteen now." He spoke gently. Carole was glad that he seemed to understand her nervousness.

"And besides, you told Max we'd get to Pine Hollow around noon," Lisa reminded her. "There's plenty of time yet."

"Uh, sure," Carole told them, but their words didn't relieve her discomfort. Now that Kate was just about to arrive, all she could think of was how foolish she'd been last week. How dumb she must have sounded.

How babyish Kate probably thought she was. How stupid. How— She cringed, just thinking about it all again.

Stevie stood up from the breakfast table, where the four of them had been lingering over coffee cake. She took her plate to the sink.

"Green car?" she asked, looking through the window. "With California plates that say KERNEL D?"

"That's it!" Carole said. She leapt up from the table, nearly upsetting a glass of milk. "I'll go get Kate!" she uttered breathlessly, heading for the door at breakneck speed.

"If my daughter ever enters the Kentucky Derby," Colonel Hanson said with a grin, "I don't believe she'll need a horse under her to win." He stood up and followed her out the door to greet their guests.

Lisa and Stevie waited patiently in the kitchen, rinsing the dishes and putting them in the dishwasher for the Hansons. They both understood that Carole needed to clear the air with Kate before anything else.

Stevie brought the final glass from the table. Lisa, standing at the sink, could see out the window. She provided the play-by-play.

"Okay, now, first Mrs. Devine steps out of the car. Colonel Hanson hugs her. Back door opens. That must be Kate. She's a knockout!" Lisa said, the envy clear in her voice. "Oh, I love those clothes!"

"I don't want to know what she's wearing. I want to know what she's doing!" Stevie complained.

"Okay, okay. Carole's waiting for her and— Listen, why don't you come watch for yourself?" Lisa invited, moving over so Stevie could look out the window, too.

AT THE HANSONS' driveway, Carole smiled nervously at Kate.

"Oh, I'm glad you could—uh—come over today," Carole said.

Kate stepped over to her uncertainly. "I feel awful," Kate said.

"Are you sick?" Carole asked.

"No, that's not what I mean," Kate said. "I did something awful to you last week at Quantico."

"You did? I thought I did something awful," Carole began. "I can't believe how stupid I must have sounded—I mean, how stupid I was. It's just that I—"

"It's all my fault. I should have told you," Kate said. "Somehow, though, when I didn't tell you right away, I just couldn't."

"But everything I said must have sounded so dumb. I was embarrassed that my father had to tell me who you are."

"I should have told you," Kate said. "I'm sorry. I'm really sorry. I hope we can still be friends."

"If you aren't mad at me because I behaved like an idiot, then everything's fine."

"Everything's fine," Kate assured her.

"Oh, good!" Carole said, grinning. "Come on in the house. Stevie and Lisa are here. They're just dying to meet you."

Carole picked up Kate's overnight bag and led her in through the kitchen door.

"Kate, I'd like you to meet my two best friends," Carole announced. "This is Stevie Lake and this is Lisa Atwood."

Lisa felt a little awkward in the presence of somebody she'd heard so much about.

"Boy, I'm glad to meet you two," Kate said brightly, immediately breaking the ice and putting Stevie and Lisa at ease. "Carole couldn't stop talking about you last week, so I feel as if I already know you."

Suddenly, Kate Devine didn't seem so much like royalty to Lisa. She seemed more like a regular person. And whatever had caused the misunderstanding between Kate and Carole seemed to have been resolved. Lisa knew that she and Stevie would have to wait to learn the full story.

"Come on, I'll show you my room," Carole said, leading the way up the stairs.

As they climbed upstairs, Lisa noticed again how well Kate was dressed. She was wearing stylishly cut jeans, topped by an oversize red-and-white-striped cotton shirt that seemed to show off her nice figure. Her deep auburn hair was held in a ponytail by a ribbon that matched the pattern of her shirt. Her shoes, though just casual sports shoes, were the same red-and-white. On her left wrist, she wore a bright red-and-white watch. Somehow, even with perfectly normal casual clothes and patterns, Kate managed to look very specially dressed. The word was style, and Kate had it.

"Well, we feel as if we know you, too," Stevie told Kate when they got to Carole's room. "Because if you think Carole talked a lot about *us* last weekend, you should have heard what she's been saying about *you* all week!"

Kate smiled warmly. "I sure hope I won't be a disappointment," she said.

"No way," Lisa assured her. "Not if you're half as neat as Carole says."

Kate grinned at her warm welcome. "Well, I'm glad to be here. I like seeing 'real' towns."

Lisa and Stevie looked at her quizzically.

"She means like a town that's *not* a military base," Carole translated, flopping onto her bed. Kate sat down beside her.

"Right. Bases are nice in a way," Kate told the girls. "For example, they are really *clean*."

"Sure, you can be court-martialed for dropping a gum wrapper, right?" Stevie teased.

"Almost," Carole said, grinning. "Anyway, the total effect isn't at all the same as a civilian town. The total effect on a military base is, well, military."

"I couldn't have said it better myself," Kate said, laughing. "So, now what am I going to get to see in this real town?" she asked Carole.

"Dad told me that he wanted to visit with your parents, show them around a bit, but that we can go to Pine Hollow—that is, if you'd like."

Lisa noticed Carole was being a bit more timid than

usual. She was clearly awed by Kate, and it was out of character for Carole to be awed by anybody, especially when it came to horses. Carole continued, "I hope you don't mind, but I told Max—he's our teacher—that we'd be there. He said he'd really like to meet you. The only trouble is that usually the summer campers, like us, have trouble riding there on weekends. See, the horses are all reserved, so it's hard to ride. But there's lots to see—including Samson, the brand-new foal."

"He's the one you three delivered, right?" Kate asked.

"Actually, it seemed that Delilah did most of the work," Stevie told her. "But we're sort of his aunts, you know?"

"Yeah, I know," Kate said. "And I love foals. There was one at one of the bases . . ." she began.

After Kate had put her clothes for the weekend in Carole's closet, all four of the girls headed to the Hansons' patio, still chatting about horses. While Kate spoke, Lisa began thinking how much she liked this girl—how right Carole had been. It was as if the four of them had been together talking about horses for months, maybe years.

". . . She was a wonderful horse. She'd ride all day for you, until she dropped. But, believe me, she would go at her own pace. There was no fire in her at all!"

Stevie, Lisa, and Carole all laughed at Kate's story. "That's not like our Samson. At least I don't think so.

He was standing and nursing within a few minutes. That one has fire!" Stevie told her.

"He sounds so cute," Kate said. "I can't wait to see him."

"Maybe Dad's ready to take us over to Pine Hollow," Carole said, standing up to find her father.

"DON'T FORGET TO show Kate the tack room," Stevie said a half hour later, tugging at Carole's sleeve. The four girls were about to enter the stable at Pine Hollow. "After all, we polished everything in the joint just in your honor!"

"You're kidding!" Kate said. "No dusty saddles? No dingy bridles? It won't seem like a real stable."

"Okay," Carole agreed with Stevie. "We'll start in the tack room. Almost everything is polished, but it's only partly in your honor. The fact is, there's going to be a three-day event here in a couple of weeks and everything needs to be totally shiny for that. We're also having a gymkhana for us—you know, the young riders. You're going to love it, too. Just wait!"

Carole led Kate into the tack room. On the walls and the saddle racks, everything was lined up carefully, and glowingly clean. The air was filled with the wonderful pungent smells of clean leather and horses. In one corner, a few kittens tumbled playfully, batting around an S-hook and chasing after it.

"Looks just like a tack room!" Kate remarked. "Oh,

except that the tack is noticeably cleaner than in any other tack room I've ever seen."

Kate was joking, but Lisa could see Carole flush with pleasure. All of the members of The Saddle Club were proud of Pine Hollow. It was the kind of place where everybody pitched in to do the work, so everybody could be proud of her accomplishments.

"And here's the locker area. We each have a little cubby where we can stow our stuff. And for riders who don't have their own hats—" Carole turned to gesture toward the wall where the hats were kept. The wall was covered with tenpenny nails spaced a few inches apart to hold a variety of sizes of black velvet-covered regulation riding hats. "—here are—"

Carole paused. She realized with a start that the riding caps were not scattered on the nails randomly, as usual. In fact, they were very carefully arranged so that they formed the letters K-A-T-E!

"Oh!" Kate said, surprised. "Now I *do* feel welcome!"

Carole's eyes went to Stevie. "Do I see your fine hand here?" she asked. Stevie grinned, acknowledging responsibility. "Sometimes Stevie uses the hats for a message board," Carole explained.

"Well, thanks, Stevie," Kate said.

"You're welcome—and I mean *very* welcome. We're glad to have you at Pine Hollow."

"I'm just a visitor," Kate reminded her.

Lisa hoped that Kate wouldn't be *just* a visitor for long, and she could tell that her friends were hoping the same thing.

Carole took Kate on the extended grand tour of the stable. The group paused at almost every stall for an introduction to each horse. Kate listened and seemed to enjoy the tour, but Lisa noticed that although she appeared interested in Pine Hollow, she didn't offer any information about her own riding experience. It was almost as if she were avoiding the topic. Lisa wondered why that would be. She decided to try the direct approach.

"What kind of horse do you ride in competition?" Lisa asked.

"Oh, different ones," Kate said evasively.

"Thoroughbreds?" Lisa asked.

"Sometimes," Kate answered.

Stevie and Carole both asked Kate questions about the horse shows she'd ridden in and the prizes she'd won, and each time they got the same kind of evasive answer Lisa had gotten. It was clear that the door was shut. The girls knew better than to pry.

"And now it's time to meet Samson," Carole said, leading the group to the paddock where the three-week-old foal was frisking about.

"Oh, he's beautiful!" Kate said, all reserve melting away. "Look how long his legs are—and his coat is so shiny already!"

"Come on up this way," Carole said. "We can sit on

this knoll here and watch, but we're far enough away so that Delilah feels secure."

The four girls walked up the hill and sat comfortably on the dry grass, warmed by the summer sun. A breeze brought the fresh scent of hay and horses to them. Carole thought that the sight of horses at play and the scent of fresh fields were the nicest treats she could give her senses.

Delilah had eyed the visitors warily while they stood at the edge of the paddock, glancing back and forth between the girls and her foal. But when the girls moved back to the knoll and sat down, she seemed to relax, confident that there was no danger to her baby.

"She's something," Carole said. "I've been riding her for a couple of years now and she's terrific with me. As a rider, she trusts me completely. But now that she's a mother—"

"Mares are very different when they are with newborns," Kate agreed. "She'll relax a little bit as Samson grows up. And I'm sure that when you ride her again, she'll be just as trusting—as long as she knows Samson's okay."

"Mothers are like that," Lisa agreed, thinking of her own occasionally overbearing, overprotective mother. "And speaking of mothers, I promised mine I'd be home in time for lunch." She stood up and glanced at Stevie.

"Me, too," Stevie said, rising as well. "Carole, thanks for the great time last night." She looked at

Kate. "Get her to make popcorn, Kate. She's the *best* at it. I'm glad you've come to Pine Hollow. We're going to have fun together," Stevie added.

"Thanks," Kate said.

"So long," Lisa told Kate and Carole. Then, waving good-bye, she and Stevie headed down the knoll. As they neared the barn, Carole could hear Stevie talking.

"About last night . . ." Stevie said, "I feel bad about not setting your hair right. I've got a crimper at home. I could bring it over to your place and we could try that—"

Lisa just gave Stevie a withering look. Then they both burst into laughter.

From where she sat, Carole laughed, too, and then she explained the joke to Kate.

"Your friends are really nice," Kate said.

"Yeah, and you're going to love riding with them," Carole told her.

Kate was quiet for a moment. Her eyes were on the black colt and his mother, but Carole knew her mind was somewhere else. Idly, Kate plucked a long stalk of grass from the knoll and chewed on the end of it.

"Carole," Kate began with a sigh, "I don't ride anymore."

"Well, I know it can be tough sometimes when your dad is stationed at a base without horses, but once you're moved into Willow Creek, you'll be able to come to Pine Hollow."

"No, that's not what I mean. I mean that no matter where we live, I don't want to ride anymore. I've told my parents. I told them after my last show."

"But you're good enough to go to the top!" Carole said, astonished by Kate's announcement.

"Maybe," Kate said.

"Just because you lost one show doesn't mean you should quit!"

"But I didn't lose," Kate said. "I took a first in three events, a second place in two. I've got a wall full of ribbons and a cabinet of silver cups. I'm no loser."

Carole shook her head in confusion. "I don't understand," she said. "I mean, I decided to quit riding once, when Samson's father had to be put down and I thought the world had come to an end. But after a while, I realized that I just loved horses too much."

"I love horses, too. That won't stop. It's riding I don't like."

Kate stared thoughtfully at the sky and continued chewing on the stalk of grass. Carole waited. There were times to ask questions. But Carole sensed this was a time to wait, so she watched the foal until Kate was ready to speak.

Samson flicked his tiny tail furiously, trying to get rid of an annoying fly, but the fly apparently was unimpressed with the colt's efforts and kept pestering him. Wisely, Samson sidled over to his mother. As soon as Delilah spotted the fly, she brushed her long tail around her foal's hindquarters, and the fly retreated.

"I've done all the riding I ever want to do," Kate said finally. "I know how *you* feel. I know how much *I* used to love riding, but I don't anymore. I'm done with it. Period."

How could anything be that final? Carole wondered. *How could such a thing have happened at all?*

ON MONDAY MORNING, Stevie and Lisa were eager to talk to Carole. They wanted to hear all about the rest of her visit with Kate.

"Oh, she's so neat!" Lisa said. "I really like her. And her clothes. You know, there's just something about the way she walks and talks. She's older than we are, but not much. She's only fourteen, but she's so grown-up!"

"I think you grow up fast on the competition circuit," Carole said. "We talked about it a little, and she said it's like you're always on display. Actually, she didn't really want to talk about riding." She looked at her friends seriously. "In fact, she's quit."

"Quit?! How could somebody so good—a champion—quit?" Stevie asked.

"She didn't want to talk about *why*, but she's definitely made up her mind. And, she's determined."

"Hah!" Stevie huffed. Lisa and Carole looked at her. "This sounds to me like a job for The Saddle Club!"

"What are you talking about?" Carole asked.

"We'll just have to show her how wrong she is," Stevie said.

"Come on, you can't interfere with somebody else's life," Carole told her.

"Oh, yes you can!" Stevie retorted. "When you see somebody making a *terrible* mistake, and it's your friend, well, you'd just *better* interfere. That's what we do for each other, isn't it? I mean belonging to The Saddle Club means helping friends—even when they don't know they need your help."

"But Kate isn't *in* The Saddle Club," Carole reminded Stevie.

"Not yet," Stevie said.

"I think I'm beginning to like this idea," Lisa said. She looked at Carole for a reaction.

"I don't know," Carole said. "But I guess it's worth a try. And experience shows that when we three work together—"

"Just what I had in mind." Max Regnery's deep, booming voice interrupted them. "You girls have been nagging me for weeks about being on the same team at the gymkhana. Well, I'm going to grant your wish. I want to see what you three *can* accomplish together."

"Oh, wow!" Stevie said. "We won't let you down,

Max! We'll be terrific. We'll probably win all the prizes."

"That's not what I have in mind for you to accomplish."

The three girls got a queasy feeling. Max had a way of getting his riders to do things they never thought they could, just because he told his students he expected them to be able to.

"Just what do you want us to accomplish?" Stevie asked.

"The gymkhana teams each have four riders on them. Your team now has three, and you are all good riders. In order to even up the teams, you need a fourth. I'm assigning the newest, greenest rider in the stable to your team as well. I want you girls to work with the new rider closely, and cooperatively. Can you do it?"

"Well, sure," Carole said. "We always help the new girls." She spoke eagerly, until she caught the grim look on Stevie's face. Max's next words confirmed her friend's apparent suspicions.

"This one isn't a girl," he said. "It's a boy, and his name is Chad Lake." He paused while the full weight of his pronouncement sank in. "In fact, here he comes now, girls. Why don't you help him get ready for class. He's had an awful lot of trouble with his tack."

"That's an understatement," Stevie grumbled. "He's been here a week and he *still* can't tell a halter from a bridle!"

"Yes, he'll be a challenge for you," Max said matter-of-factly. "But I'm sure you're up to it. See you in class. Fifteen minutes now. Don't be late."

Chad sauntered up to his sister and her friends. "Good morning, teammates!" he greeted them.

"Oh, groan!" Stevie said.

"Come on, Stevie," Carole said. "Let's get ready for class. You promised to help me check Diablo's hooves for pebbles."

"I did?" Stevie asked, confused.

"Definitely," Carole said, grabbing Stevie's sleeve and yanking her through the tack room toward the other aisle of horses.

"What were you talking about?" Stevie hissed at Carole when they were out of Lisa and Chad's earshot.

"If you're busy with me, then *Lisa* can help Chad," Carole explained.

"Ooooh, I *get* it," Stevie said, seeing the light. "But what's wrong with Diablo's hooves?"

"Nothing," Carole said, rolling her eyes. "Let's just get ready for class, okay?"

"HERE, CHAD," LISA said. "Remember now how to hold the bridle while you're putting it on? You have to kind of reach up under the horse's neck—"

Chad stood next to Patch, the bridle dangling awkwardly from his outstretched hands. Patch had a look in his eye that said "No way."

"Right, then first, the bit," Chad said.

"Uh-uh," Lisa corrected him. "Bring the crownpiece up first with your right hand, and then . . ." Her voice trailed off because there was no point in continuing. Chad had dropped the crownpiece and was grasping the bit. The whole bridle was a tangle. Patch blinked his eyes languidly. If he could have spoken, Lisa was sure his words would have been "Give me a break."

"I guess I'd better do it for you," Lisa said, reaching for the tangle of leather. "You watch, though, so you can do it yourself next time."

"I'll try," Chad promised while Lisa deftly slid the bit into the horse's mouth and then slipped the crownpiece over his ears. "I'll really try. I just don't seem to have much aptitude for this, though, you know?"

"You'll learn," Lisa assured him, buckling the final straps on the bridle. "It's just a matter of time. This stuff was really confusing for me, too, at first. Pretty soon, you'll get good at it."

"Maybe," Chad said, taking the reins from her. While he held the horse, she tightened up the girth. "Um, Lisa," Chad began. "Would you like to go to a movie, or something, like after riding tomorrow?"

With a start, Lisa realized that Chad had just asked her out on a date. Her mind raced. *A date.* She could wear her favorite pink top over the denim skirt and the sandals her mother had bought for her—but they were yellow and that didn't go at all. . . . Flushing with embarrassment, Lisa realized Chad was waiting for her to answer him.

"Me?" she said, her heart beating so fast she was sure he could hear it.

"Yeah, you," he assured her.

"Well, sure," she said, suddenly grinning. "I'd like that."

"Great," Chad said. "There's a neat movie at the Triplex. We can just walk over from here after we're done."

So much for my pink top and denim skirt, Lisa thought to herself. She was going on her first date in riding clothes. Well, what did that matter? At least she was *going* on it.

"What's the movie?" Lisa asked.

"*Revenge of the Mummy, Part Six.* Did you see the other parts?"

"No," Lisa said, shaking her head. "I'm afraid I missed them."

"I'll tell you about them," Chad said. Lisa opened Patch's stall so that Chad could lead his horse toward the indoor ring, where his class was about to begin.

"I can't wait," Lisa said.

"So far, my favorite was *Part Three*," Chad told her. "That was the one where the archaeologist gets trapped in the ancient burial room with these bones, see, and he thinks they're just bones, but it turns out—"

"All beginner students proceed to the indoor ring!" Mrs. Reg's voice boomed over the P.A. "Class is about to begin."

"Hey, that's me," Chad said. "See you later, okay?"

"Right, later," Lisa said. She watched the horse and rider walk away toward the ring.

Revenge of the Mummy, Part Six? Lisa said to herself. *How could there be six parts of a revenge? Of a mummy? How could somebody care—six times?*

It was time for her to get Pepper ready for class, and Max wouldn't like it if she was late. She hurried to the tack room, collected her horse's gear, and carried it back to Pepper's stall. By the time she'd gotten the bridle on, she had succeeded in convincing herself that if somebody nice, say Chad, liked mummy movies, maybe she'd really been missing something all along. She decided to keep an open mind.

9

"CHAD, IF YOU don't hold the spoon level, the egg is never going to stay on it," Stevie said in total exasperation.

It was Tuesday, and Chad and The Saddle Club girls were trying to practice for the gymkhana. Every time Chad did something wrong, Stevie got crankier and crankier. Lisa was feeling very uncomfortable with the whole situation. As soon as this practice was over, she and Chad were going to the movies. The problem was that Lisa hadn't told Carole or Stevie about it, and she was sure Chad hadn't mentioned it to Stevie. It wasn't exactly being dishonest with her best friends, but, she had to tell herself, it wasn't telling the truth, either.

Chad came bounding up on his pony, Half Dollar, to where Lisa stood at the far end of the ring, and stuck out a spoon. Lisa supplied him with the egg for the gymkhana practice—which he promptly dropped.

"Big deal," Chad grumbled as Stevie rolled her eyes at him.

"It *is* a big deal to us," Stevie told her brother. "Now try it again."

Once again, Chad turned his pony and retreated to the starting line. Carole, aboard Quarter, gave the signal to start. Chad told Half Dollar to "giddyup," which inspired the pony to a grudging walk. Carole clicked her tongue until the pony broke into a trot. Chad, surprised by the sudden speed, nearly tumbled off the back end of his pony.

"Hold on!" Stevie yelled. Chad grabbed the pony's mane at the moment he broke into a canter. As the pony approached the table where Lisa stood ready to hand out an egg, Chad managed to slow Half Dollar down. Chad thrust a spoon at Lisa and she slid another egg onto it. He nudged the pony with his heels and once again Half Dollar spurted. The egg dropped off Chad's spoon about ten feet from the finish line.

"Better, definitely better," Carole said optimistically.

"But not good enough," Stevie complained. "It's a good thing we hard-boiled these eggs. We couldn't possibly afford to use all the raw eggs Chad would break. At least we can recycle the cracked ones."

Chad glared at his sister. "Speaking of 'cracked ones,'" he began in a threatening tone.

"I think it's time to concentrate on a different event," Carole interrupted. "How about the water-gun race?"

"Fine," Stevie grumbled. "The water's free around here."

"And besides, I'm good at the water-gun race," Chad said. "Are we going to be finished soon? Our movie starts at four."

"Are we going to the movies?" Stevie glanced at her watch. "Well, we really have to give these poor ponies a rest. We'll quit at three-fifteen. What movie did you want to see?"

"Not you and me, Stevie," Chad said. "You're not invited. I invited Lisa to come to the movies."

Stevie and Carole looked at Lisa, raising their eyebrows. She squirmed uncomfortably until Stevie spoke.

"No problem, Chad," she said. "We can stop right after we go once through the water-gun race. That should give you plenty of time."

Lisa sighed with relief. If Stevie or Carole had been annoyed that she'd kept her secret about Chad, they would have said something immediately—at least Stevie would have. The fact was, Lisa didn't quite know how she felt about the whole idea herself. It was exciting to think of having a date, but she'd argued with her mother for what had seemed like hours on Monday just to get permission to spend two hours with a boy in a movie theater!

In the next fifteen minutes, the girls and Chad all practiced with the squirt gun and the target on horseback. Just as Chad had promised, he *was* very good at it. Somehow, he managed to hit the target, even while he was wobbling around in the pony's saddle.

"You've got to have a good steady stream of water to be able to aim it," he told the girls. "So squeeze hard, okay?"

Lisa tried it, but no matter how hard she squeezed, she couldn't get the water anywhere near the target. Carole and Stevie were a little disappointed, but that made them more or less even since Lisa was the best of the team at the egg race.

When they'd finished practice, they took their ponies back to their stalls, untacked them, and cooled them down. Stevie brought a bucket of fresh water into Penny's stall, where Lisa was brushing her quickly.

"Here," Stevie said, hooking the bucket onto the wall, where Penny could reach it. "I don't want you to be late for your date."

Lisa looked at Stevie uncertainly. "You don't mind, do you?" she asked.

Stevie grinned and shook her head. "I guess if I had a date with someone like my brother, I'd keep it a secret, too," she teased. "But aside from that, how could I mind? It's *so* exciting that I'm almost jealous." She gave Lisa a little hug. "What movie are you seeing?" she asked.

"Well . . ." Lisa began as she stuck the brush into her

pocket and stepped out of the stall. Stevie followed, sliding the door closed behind her and latching it carefully. "We're seeing *Revenge of the Mummy, Part Six.*"

"I take it back," Stevie said. "I'm not jealous at all."

Lisa burst into giggles and Stevie joined her.

They were still laughing when they arrived at the locker area.

"Ready to go?" Chad asked brightly.

Lisa nodded, and they were off.

THE MOVIE THEATER was within walking distance of Pine Hollow, so at least they didn't have to rely on anyone's parent to drive them. Lisa had promised her mother she'd be home by six-thirty, though what her mother was so worried about wasn't really clear to Lisa.

Lisa had been anticipating her first date for a long time. She was an organized person, a list maker, so it wasn't surprising that she had made lists of things she could talk about on her first date. Somehow, the idea of awkward silences had filled her with terror. As it turned out, she had no such problem with Chad.

"Did you go out for a sport last year?" she asked (Item Number One on her list of conversation topics).

"Yeah," he said, and then abandoned the subject altogether. "Now let me tell you about what happened in the last movie because it may be really important to what's going on in this one, though probably not since that was a couple of years ago. But, see, this archaeologist was trying to break into the tomb of the king of someplace, I don't remember where, but it doesn't matter because it's this ancient cult, see? And the curse is that if somebody lets light fall on the casket, he'll get it from the mummy—I mean the mummy of the king's bodyguard, not the king. He's actually dead."

"Isn't the bodyguard dead, too?" Lisa asked.

"Well, sure, but see, it's his curse to return to life if somebody disturbs his master's grave."

"Oh."

"So then he . . ." Lisa listened with growing concern as Chad described an impossibly complicated but otherwise mindless plot. The more he talked, the more enthralled he became and the more worried Lisa became.

"You really like this?" Lisa asked finally, interrupting his monologue.

"Oh, yeah, it's cool. You'll see," he assured her, but Lisa didn't feel the least bit assured.

When they got to the Triplex, Chad paid for her ticket, but he let her buy the popcorn and soda. Lisa liked it that they could share expenses. Then, with some trepidation on Lisa's part, they went into the darkened theater and Lisa settled into her soft seat to learn the fate of the greedy archaeologist who would awaken the evil spirit of the mummy. Once again Chad assured her she was really going to like the movie.

She still wasn't feeling assured when it began. The mummy, it seemed, had built up a lot of anger over the course of the first five movies, so his thirst for revenge was considerable. Lisa squirmed uncomfortably in her seat while the tension built and, as the bloody battles began, she tried scrunching down in her seat. Chad tugged at her sleeve.

"Don't miss this part coming up," he hissed, pulling her back up in her seat. Reluctantly, she sat up, but she found that she could close her eyes and Chad wouldn't notice, since his own were glued to the screen, where the mummy was wreaking his terrible revenge.

Finally, it was more than Lisa could take. She had to get out of there. "Chad," she whispered, "I'm not too crazy about this."

"It's going to get even more exciting now, just you see," he said.

But it didn't. The mummy just figured out creative things to do with sharp pieces of broken pottery.

"I think I'd better go," she said.

"Didn't you go before the movie started?" he asked.

"No, not go like that," she said. "Go, like *go*. I don't like this at all. I don't want to watch any more."

"You lost your watch?" he asked, clearly distracted.

"No, I'm *leaving*," she said. "I'll wait for you outside. Here, you take the popcorn," she told him. She climbed over him to the aisle, and escaped to the lobby.

In the rest room, Lisa ran a comb through her hair,

applied some lip gloss, and looked herself straight in the eye. Since all three movies playing at the Triplex had just begun, the rest room was mercifully empty, so she could have a serious conversation with herself.

"Yikes!" she began. "That is the most awful, boring, gory movie I have ever seen and ever want to see." Saying it out loud made her feel a little better. Ever since Chad had told her his choice of movie, she'd felt uneasy, and now she knew she'd been right.

Chad was sweet in his way. She'd liked the way he'd asked her out, and she'd liked the way he'd announced to Carole and Stevie that they were going out. He wasn't in the least bit uncomfortable with it and that was nice. She'd been more ill at ease with her friends than he had been.

The problem was that Chad was nice enough, but he'd made a terrible mistake with her; if this was the kind of movie he liked, there was no way she'd ever go out with him again. At the same time, it was as clear to Lisa as it had been to her friends that Chad's motive in joining the riding class was to be near her. He didn't seem to like riding much more than she liked horror movies.

But there were other things she liked, she reminded herself. She liked ballet, she liked reading and schoolwork. Maybe the two of them had other areas of common interest. Common Interest was something she'd read a lot about in articles about dating. It was important for boys and girls who were dating to have Common Interests. *Otherwise*—Lisa sighed, looking at herself in the mirror once again—*the girl will spend all their movie dates in the rest room, pretending her hair needs a combing, and the boy will spend all their horseback-riding dates pretending he cares which end of the horse goes first.*

"What we have here," Lisa said, once again addressing the mirror, "is a serious lack of Common Interests."

Lisa returned to the lobby of the theater. The movie would be over in twenty minutes now, so she would just wait for Chad. There was no way she could return to the scene of the chaos in the mummy's tomb. In the meantime, she had twenty minutes to figure out how to tell Chad she didn't want to go to another movie with him.

As it turned out, it wasn't necessary at all. Chad came bounding out of the theater with worry written on his face. As soon as he spotted her, she stood up.

"You didn't come back," he said. "I guess you didn't much like it, huh? I'm sorry."

"Chad, I have the feeling I liked it about as much as you like horseback riding," she said.

His face flushed with embarrassment. "You could tell?" he asked. She nodded. "I thought if somebody as nice as you liked it, I would, too," he said. "Even though Stevie likes it," he quickly added.

"That's what I thought about the movie when you first told me what you wanted to see."

"No fun for you at all?"

"None," she told him honestly.

"Well, I guess we were both wrong. I won't convert you to mummy movies, and you won't convert me to horseback riding. Since you know why I did it and everybody knows how bad I am at it, I'll just drop out."

Lisa nodded absently, more than a little sad that both of their plans had failed. This wasn't the kind of first date she'd been dreaming about for so long. First dates were supposed to be fun. It didn't seem fair.

"I'll just clear out my locker at the stable tomorrow," Chad continued.

"What do you mean, clear out your locker?" Lisa asked. What Chad had said about quitting had finally registered.

"It's time for me to quit riding," he explained.

For a second, Lisa was going to agree with him, but then she remembered what would happen if he *did* quit riding. It would break up The Saddle Club's gymkhana team. It might even mean they'd have to drop out altogether, since *all* the students were now assigned to teams, and, like theirs, had probably been practicing already as teams.

"You can't do that!" she burst out.

"Why not?"

She explained what would happen with their team and how awful that would be, especially since his own sister had practically invented the gymkhana for the stable.

Chad's face fell. "But I'm so awful at it."

That was certainly true. He *wasn't* very good and Lisa was tempted to agree with him, but the fact was that no matter how he rode, and dropped eggs, he was better than nothing. This was going to call for some diplomacy.

"Chad," she began, "all of the teams have been carefully balanced with experienced and inexperienced riders. Although no two riders have the same skills, the teams are as equal as Max could make them."

"You mean that because Carole is the best rider at the stable, your team got me—the worst?"

"I didn't say that," she said.

"You didn't have to."

"Listen—you can stop riding anytime you want to. After the gymkhana. Until then, you're going to have to stick with us. Besides, you may not be much on a horse, but you're absolutely terrific with a water pistol. How do you do it?"

"Years of practice," he told her, and she knew it was true. Water pistols, mummy movies. Chad was a nice boy, but he wasn't for her.

They left the theater together and began walking home. Since they lived near each other, they had about fifteen minutes to chat. Lisa quickly exhausted her list of conversation topics. Chad dismissed each in turn with a shrug or an okay. Finally, she resigned herself to letting him tell her the plot of the movie she'd just missed.

Her occasional nods and uh-huhs seemed to satisfy him and freed her to ponder her failed first date. If this was a date, she really wasn't looking forward to her second. She'd enjoyed her anticipation of her first date, though. Why should she let all that fun daydreaming go to waste? If this time with Chad was such a bust, then it couldn't possibly be a date. That meant that she still had her first date to look forward to!

That was something to smile about. She was grinning with her secret by the time she and Chad went their different ways. Very different ways.

LISA, CAROLE, AND Stevie were each assigned a different chore the next morning. Afterward, while Carole and Stevie were in their jumping class, Lisa was on the trail with the newer riders. The girls didn't have a minute to talk with one another until lunchtime.

Carole and Stevie were practically bursting with curiosity by the time they sat down together on the knoll overlooking Samson's paddock. They waited expectantly while Lisa removed the foil top from her yogurt and opened up her fruit juice. Stevie tore the foil off her peanut-butter-and-honey sandwich, keeping her eyes on Lisa all the while. Carole munched on a celery stalk, watching too.

"Well?" Carole said finally.

Lisa sighed. "It was a mistake," she said simply. "We

went to the movie, which was awful, as far as I was concerned, but he *loved* it. I tried to talk about things that interest me. He couldn't care less. What I mean is that it just wasn't any fun."

"What you mean is that my brother's not good enough for you!" Stevie said in a huff.

Carole looked at her in astonishment. "You're defending your brother—the one you've called a jerk, dweeb, creep, and idiot, to name just a few—in our hearing?"

Stevie blushed. "Well, but he's *my* brother. I can call him those names. Nobody else can." She looked at Lisa accusingly.

"Nobody else did," Carole reminded her.

"And that's not the way I felt about him," Lisa said. "He was really nice to me, and I was nice to him. But I don't think that's what a date is supposed to be like. We just didn't have anything in common."

Stevie cooled off as quickly as she'd heated up. She was like that, and her friends knew it. Lisa started describing the afternoon with Chad and, by the time she'd gotten to the second episode of gruesome murder in the pharaoh's tomb, Stevie was giggling.

"Oh, he has the most rotten taste in movies!" she admitted. "Okay, so he's not your dream date. Now you know why he's such a pain as a brother."

"You said it, not me!" Lisa teased. "Anyway, I accomplished one really important thing yesterday." She explained that Chad had wanted to quit riding and how she had convinced him to stick with it through the gymkhana.

"A mixed blessing," Stevie said.

"Not at all!" Carole told her. "We would be eliminated without him. Max told us that the teams are absolutely final. There are no extra riders at all. In fact, Max is trying to find somebody to help with the setup for the gymkhana. Know anybody who might be interested?"

Almost all gymkhana races and games required a lot of props, like eggs, water, targets, and hooks. Unless there were people who could help lay out the props, it could take ten times as long to set up the races as to run them.

"I could ask my brother Alex," Stevie said, and then grimaced. "On second thought, I've got enough brothers in on this deal now, haven't I?"

Carole and Lisa nodded, grinning. The three girls ate their lunches quietly, thinking. As Lisa finished her last spoonful of yogurt, her eyes lit up.

"I've got it!" she said. "Kate! I bet Kate would help. Even though she doesn't want to ride anymore, she said she still liked being around horses, didn't she, Carole?"

"Hey, that's a *wonderful* idea," Stevie chimed in. The broad smile on Carole's face signaled agreement.

"I'll call her tonight," Carole said. "The minute I get home." She finished her vegetables and began eating her salad. "You know, there's something funny going on here," she told her friends.

"No more smart remarks about my brother," Stevie joked. "That's for me to do, right?"

"Well, not exactly a smart remark about your brother," Carole said. "But what's funny has to do with him. Here we have two people, Chad and Kate. One of them—if you will excuse me saying so, Stevie—has no business being at Pine Hollow, and the other one has no business *not* being at Pine Hollow. Everything is upside down."

Stevie and Lisa nodded in agreement.

"Well, pretty soon, Chad will leave," Lisa reminded her.

"And since we've pledged to do our best to get Kate back riding again, maybe we can turn something else rightside up," Stevie said. "When the three of us team up to do something, it seems like we've got a lot of power. We can accomplish almost anything!" she announced triumphantly.

"Maybe it is us," Carole agreed philosophically. "But maybe it's really horse power."

As CAROLE HAD promised, she called Kate that night to ask if she would lend a hand with the gymkhana. At first Kate just said no.

"Well, I guess I can understand," Carole said. "It's a lot of work and not much fun, but I wanted to talk to you anyway, so I thought I'd ask."

"What did you want to talk with me about?" Kate asked, curious.

"Oh, right. It's a problem I've been having with one of the ponies—the one I'm supposed to ride for the gymkhana."

Suddenly, Kate was interested. "Tell me about it," she said.

"I can get him to move his legs *faster*," Carole explained, "but I'm having trouble getting him to lengthen his strides." This was a fairly common problem, and a relatively simple one when a horse was being a little lazy. The best way to have any horse pace efficiently was to have him take longer steps so that each stride covered more ground. For example, the difference between a slow trot and a fast trot was often more a difference between the length of the strides than the number of them.

Carole was fibbing to Kate. She wasn't having any trouble with this at all on her pony, but she wanted to get Kate involved, even if only on the telephone. Carole knew that there were a lot of ways to get a horse to lengthen his stride, and that Kate would have lots of ideas for her.

They traded ideas back and forth for about ten minutes, trying to decide on the best approach with this particular pony. Finally, Kate said, "Look, I'll be there tomorrow to help with the setup and if you're still having a problem, we can work on it together, okay? I think the most important thing is for the pony to take you seriously, you know? You're going to have to keep a leg on him and encourage him to use all his horse power for you."

"I'm sure you're right, Kate," Carole said, giggling to herself that Kate had used the very words she'd used earlier. "I think I can get him to respond more now. Thanks for the suggestions."

"No problem," Kate said cheerfully. "Glad to help. See you tomorrow afternoon."

Carole cradled the phone and smiled to herself. She knew that Kate's life was Kate's life and if Kate didn't want to ride anymore, well, that was her decision. In the meantime, however, Carole was determined to change Kate's mind for her, and she had a feeling it was going to work.

She lay back on her bed lazily and stared up at the ceiling. Snowball jumped up on the foot of the bed, sat down, and stared at her.

"You're the one who gave me the idea," Carole informed the kitten. "Sometimes when you want somebody to do something, you have to start them out in the wrong direction first, right, Snowball?"

She tapped her stomach to encourage the kitten to come closer so she could pat him. Snowball stood up and hopped down off the bed.

"Just what I mean," Carole said.

SOMEHOW, JUST HAVING Kate Devine at their next gymkhana practice seemed to make things go a little smoother. Not only did she have good suggestions for all of them on how to ride better, but she also knew some of the tricks of the trade when it came to gymkhanas.

"Hey, coach!" Stevie said. "Any pointers for the costume race?"

"Oh, sure," Kate said. "The problem with the costume race is that you have to get off your pony to put on the costume and then get back up again. You want that to be as easy as possible, so try lengthening your stirrups a couple of inches."

Each of them tried that and it did save mounting and dismounting time.

"I think I feel a blue ribbon in my future," Carole said, "thanks to you, that is."

"Did I hear someone say 'blue ribbon'?" Max asked as he strode into the ring, where they were practicing.

"We're just dreaming, Max," Lisa explained.

"Well, you're certainly working hard enough on it," he said. "Dreaming that way can get results." That sounded like a compliment to the team members, and since compliments from Max were as rare as July frosts, they were pleased. "Anyway," he continued, "I thought you'd like to know that I've just accepted a challenge from Watermill Stables. Our best gymkhana team will compete against their best as well as other local teams. Think you are up to it?" he asked.

"Oh, sure! When do we go?" Stevie asked, almost breathless with excitement.

"I don't know that *you* will," he said. "The team that wins here will go there. Think you can win here?"

The girls answered with a resounding "Yes!" Chad looked dubious, very dubious, Lisa noticed.

"We'd better get back to work right away," Carole told her friends as Max returned to his office.

The team hopped back on their ponies and resumed their practice. It went pretty smoothly this time, except when Chad kept dropping eggs, and when Lisa couldn't hit the target with her water gun, and when Stevie's pony kept wandering in circles when they were trying pin-the-tail-on-the-pony, and when Carole kept tripping over her pirate sword in the costume race.

On the whole, things were not looking good, but Lisa was an optimist. "I think we've taken some big steps today," she reassured her friends as they walked their ponies to cool them down before stabling them for the day.

"Yeah," Stevie agreed sarcastically. "All backward."

"If you want my advice," Kate interrupted, "I suggest that you put the horses away and take the weekend off and just forget about the whole thing until Monday. Then you can start fresh."

"You mean we shouldn't even think about the gymkhana all weekend?" Lisa asked.

"Not at all," Kate told her. "Oh, well, maybe you might pick up a squirt gun at the five-and-dime and try to improve your aim, and Chad, you should try balance exercises, like—"

"Stop!" Stevie said. "I think you were right in the first place. Let's take the weekend off. Deal?"

"Deal!" they all agreed together. It was, Lisa noted, just about the first time they'd ever all agreed on anything.

11

"NOW WATCH HOW the rider brings her horse into the turn at the corner of the ring," Carole told Lisa and Stevie. The three girls were sitting in the audience at the dressage test—the first day of the three-day event. Lisa realized that she'd been so focused on their gymkhana, which would begin that afternoon, that she'd almost forgotten about the adult activities.

Dressage, as Carole had explained earlier to her, was the portion of the three-day event in which the horse's manners and training were being tested. Of course, that meant evaluating the rider's performance, too, but the horse's response to the rider's instructions was the key in this part of the competition. In a way, it was like the school-figures part of a figure-skating competition. Each of the competitors walked, trotted, and cantered her horse through the same exercise, which included diagonals, circles, and straight lines, measured precisely in the dressage ring.

"Uh-oh, look at that," Carole remarked quietly.

"What?" Lisa asked. She thought the rider was doing a pretty good job.

"Well, she let her horse slow down the pace, and now, oh, no, look at *that* corner."

Lisa watched carefully. Then she saw what Carole meant. The rider had let the horse cut the corner. "Points off, huh?"

Carole nodded.

No matter how hard Lisa watched, she couldn't see as many mistakes as Carole could. She sometimes couldn't even tell when things were being done right. Kate, sitting to her right, tried to help her see the fine points of the performances.

"See how the horse is balanced?" she asked Lisa.

Lisa tried to see it. Finally, she began to get the idea. "You mean the way his pace remains smooth and even?"

"You're getting it, Lisa, you're getting it," Kate told her. Lisa grinned, pleased with herself, and, with the help of her local experts, she began to enjoy watching the competition. For the moment she'd forgotten that her own competition, the gymkhana, would begin at four o'clock—a mere five hours away.

CAROLE WAS VERY pleased that Kate had agreed to come to the adult events. These were the types of competitions at which Kate herself had excelled. Carole wanted to see how Kate would react to watching these events. She had the feeling that Kate's participation, no matter how slight, was going to be the key to luring her back into riding. For a few moments, Carole watched Kate looking at the riders. At first, she thought she could see Kate moving with them unconsciously, sometimes shifting her own weight to turn the horse she was riding in her imagination, sometimes sitting back to slow the animal down. Then Carole realized it wasn't Kate moving that way, it was she herself. *Carole* was taking every pace with the riders. Kate was just sitting on the bench watching. Kate was still a mystery.

BY FIVE MINUTES to four, all thoughts of the dressage test were erased from the minds of the four members of the gymkhana team. Since there were four teams, Max had assigned each team the name of a suit of cards. The Saddle Club, plus Chad, had been dubbed The Clubs. That pleased the girls. Chad didn't seem to care.

In fact, Stevie noticed, Chad seemed very distracted. She and Lisa and Carole were buzzing with reminders of special techniques for the races. Chad stared across the course.

"Nervous?" Carole asked.

"Me?" Chad responded in surprise. "Nah."

"So, what's on your mind?" Carole asked him.

"My mind?"

"Why do you keep answering Carole's questions with questions?" Stevie asked him.

"Who's that?" he asked instead, pointing to Kate, who was busily setting up poles with rings on them for the riders to spear with their riding crops.

"That's Kate Devine," Lisa said, confused.

"Devine," he echoed, a sort of dreamy look in his eyes.

It seemed such an odd thing for him to say that Lisa and Carole looked to Stevie for an explanation. Stevie shook her head. "I've seen these symptoms before," she explained. "I think he just fell in love."

"But he's met her lots of times before," Carole said. "Why didn't he recognize her?"

Stevie shrugged. "Look, I can't make any more sense out of the way he falls in love with girls than I can out of the way Kate fell out of love with riding. People are people. Sometimes they make sense. Sometimes they don't. The one good piece of news here, though, is that if he's trying to show off for Kate, he'll do his best for the team."

Just then, the two-minute-warning bell rang. It was almost time.

LISA HAD BEEN in the ring where the gymkhana games were taking place dozens of times before, but somehow, everything looked very different to her now. She and her teammates were dressed in their best riding clothes. Even Stevie had abandoned her worn-out jeans and was wearing breeches and high boots. They each had a special cover on their regular riding hats to identify their team. The Clubs' caps were green-and-white. Carole's had a pompon on the top, which meant that she was the team captain, elected unanimously. That also meant that she would ride the last leg of each race and would be expected to make up time lost by the less-experienced riders who had gone before her.

The Clubs were in one of the middle lanes of the ring. Diamonds were on the far left, Spades came next, then Clubs, then Hearts. The lanes were divided by poles. Each lane had four poles, evenly spaced from the start line to the far end of the ring. In some races, the poles just divided the lanes; in others, they were either used to hold props (such as rings in the first race), or for the horses to circle or weave around. Lisa hoped she'd remember the different rules of all the races.

In fact, Lisa hoped for a lot of things. She hoped she wouldn't make any really dumb mistakes. She hoped she wouldn't fall off her pony. She hoped she wouldn't miss any targets, she hoped her pony wouldn't decide to walk all day. She hoped—she didn't have time to hope any more. The race was about to begin.

Looking to her right, Lisa spotted her parents in the crowd. Her father waved. Her mother yelled, "Be careful!" Lisa grinned to herself. It was just like her mother to be worried about her—even over such a little thing as this. It made her forget her butterflies. She was ready to go!

MRS. REG HELD her hand at shoulder level and let the red bandanna float down. As soon as it hit the ground, the race would begin. In this ring race, the first rider (Chad, on their team) was to ride to the first pole, spear a ring from it with his riding crop, circle the pole, and return to the starting line. He'd pass off the crop with the ring to their second rider (Lisa), who was to ride to the second pole, spear another ring, circle the pole, and then bring the crop back to their third rider, Stevie. And so on.

The instant the bandanna hit the ground, Chad was off like a rocket—at a walk. He kicked Half Dollar. He clucked to the pony. Nothing would move him. The girls yowled at him, but that didn't help move the pony one bit! Finally, Carole yelled at Chad, "Use the whip!" Responding quickly, Chad touched the pony lightly with the whip and the animal sprinted to the first pole. Fortunately, Chad's aim with the whip was as good as with the squirt gun. He poked the whip through the ring on the first try, and before she knew it, Lisa was grasping it from him and heading for the second pole.

It was a good thing Lisa didn't need to use the whip on her pony, because it already had one precious ring on it. If that ring fell off, they'd have to start all over again.

Penny started to turn the wrong way when Lisa got to the pole, but Lisa got her straightened out, speared the ring on the second try (better than she'd ever done in practice), and headed toward Stevie and Nickel, who were eagerly awaiting her. After she handed off the whip to Stevie, she had her first chance to see how the other teams were doing.

The Hearts were having a terrible time. Their first rider was still trying to get the ring on the whip. But the Spades were doing just fine. In fact, their third rider was almost ready to hand off the whip to their captain, but his pony lurched and all the rings fell off! They had to start all over again. Lisa watched while Kate and Red O'Malley ran frantically over to their poles to put up new rings for them. It wouldn't do for a team to lose because the setups weren't being done.

The Diamonds were running just about neck and neck with the Clubs. The Diamonds' captain was Veronica diAngelo. She was a temperamental, spoiled rich girl, but she was also a good rider. She'd give Carole a run for her money.

Veronica and Carole started their final legs at almost exactly the same second. They both leaned forward, putting pressure on their ponies to go as fast as possible. Lisa held her breath while Carole slowed Quarter ever so slightly approaching the fourth pole.

She held the reins in her left hand and the whip in her right. She pointed it as if she were aiming a rifle, looking straight ahead toward the small iron ring perched atop the striped pole.

Zip! She nailed it. The ring lifted off the top of the pole and gently slid down the whip until Carole could secure it with her fingers along with the others. Quarter picked up his pace immediately and began the mad dash for the finish line. Stevie, Lisa, and Chad all bounced up and down in their saddles, shrieking encouragement.

Veronica's team was yelling just as loud, but Lisa knew it wasn't going to do them any good at all. Veronica had missed the ring on her first try and so she had to circle the pole twice. Carole was across the finish line, waving triumphantly, by the time Veronica had gotten halfway home.

The Clubs had four points and the Diamonds had three. Hearts came in third and got two points. Poor old Spades were last. That was worth one point.

The Clubs shouted together in triumph. "We were outstanding!" Chad declared.

The girls looked at him with a little bit of surprise. It was the first time he had shown that he cared.

"I guess we were!" Lisa agreed.

"Or maybe we were just a little bit lucky—" Stevie suggested.

"You know how to find the cloudy wrapping around every lump of silver, don't you?" Carole teased her.

Stevie smiled. "I guess so. But I just don't want us to relax. After all, there are three more races today!"

"And the costume race is about to start," Carole said, glancing at the far end of the ring.

"Oh, no!" Stevie groaned. "Red has given us the clown outfit! It's got buttons up the back!"

"But who has the pirate outfit with the eyepatch?"

"The Diamonds!" Stevie said. "Can't wait to see if Veronica will allow herself to be so unchic as that!"

"She'll have to, or she'll lose," Lisa reminded her.

"She'll lose anyway!" Stevie said.

Lisa was beginning to like the feel of victory. She hoped Stevie was right.

Lisa could see her parents cheering like crazy for her, and that made her feel good all over. A lot of the time it seemed to her that her parents had trouble getting excited about the things she liked the most or did the best. She never got congratulations when she brought home a straight-A report card, but if she wasn't the butterfly in the *front* row in the ballet recital, they were disappointed. Now here they were, cheering for her as if they were really proud of her!

"There goes the bandanna!" Carole shouted, and Chad was on his way.

The costume game went smoothly for the Clubs, but it also went smoothly for the Diamonds. The Hearts and the Spades were trying their best, but they couldn't keep up with the leaders. When time permitted, the Clubs watched the other teams. It was clear that the Hearts and the Spades just hadn't put enough time in on practice. They made too many little mistakes, which wouldn't have happened if they were more familiar with the games. So, though Max had made all the teams pretty equal as far as riding ability went, when it came down to it, practice was what counted. Practice and a little bit of luck.

In the costume race, the luck went more toward the Diamonds than the Clubs. Chad accidentally ripped a hole in the leg of the clown costume when he put it on, and each of the girls stuck a leg into the hole when *she* put it on. It cost them precious seconds—enough of them that they came in second to the Diamonds. Spades came in third and Hearts, last. The Club and Diamond teams were now tied.

The third race was a disaster for the Clubs. It was a chain race, in which two riders rode side by side, holding a chain between them, weaving back and forth around the poles. For some reason, Penny suddenly decided she didn't want to have anything to do with Half Dollar. Try as Lisa and Chad did, they could barely get the ponies to stay close enough to each other so they could hold the chain. They had to start over twice. By then, the Hearts had won the race and the Diamonds had come in second. The Clubs were lucky to take third, and that meant that the Diamonds were one point ahead of them. They had to beat the Diamonds in the fourth race just to stay even for the day.

The fourth event was the squirt-gun race. It was Chad's best race, but none of the girls had ever been very good at it. Lisa was practically shaking with excitement, or nervousness. She wasn't sure which, but it didn't matter. Anything that made her shake was going to have a bad effect on her target shooting.

"Breathe deeply through your nose and out slowly through your mouth," Carole suggested to all her teammates. "It calms you and helps you focus."

"Will it help me aim?" Lisa asked.

"I'm not sure," Carole said. "But it's got to be better for you than sitting there shaking in your saddle!"

Lisa laughed, releasing tension. It felt really good. After all, these were just games, and games were for having *fun*.

"Okay, I'm ready," she announced, lining up Penny behind Half Dollar. At the far end of the ring, Kate and Red were setting up the pistol targets, cardboard cutouts set on easels. Each rider would have a separate squirt gun, with a different color dye in it. That way, there would be no arguments about who had or who had not hit the target.

The final target was balanced on an easel by the fourth pole. The teams were to ride to the line ten feet from the target and shoot. Mrs. Reg lifted her bandanna in the air and released it. It floated lazily toward the ground, landing gently, silently—in great contrast to the sudden and thunderous response from the four leadoff ponies on each of the teams.

Half Dollar, now accustomed to Chad's sudden starts, leapt from the starting line, galloped to the shooting line, and halted promptly. Without hesitation, Chad raised his right arm, took aim, and fired. Bull's-eye! Green dye smeared all over the target. Half Dollar made a U-turn and returned Chad to the starting line well ahead of the other three teams' first riders. The Clubs were ahead.

As soon as Chad crossed the line, Lisa started Penny moving. The pony followed her lead and got to the shooting line quickly. Lisa checked and found that Penny's forelegs were over the line. That would be an automatic foul. She pulled firmly on the reins until Penny stepped back behind the line. Then, looking nervously at the squirt gun in her right hand, she raised it and aimed. She squeezed the trigger. Blue dye shot from the nozzle, landing on the ground in front of the target. She squeezed again, harder. Same result.

"Higher!" she heard Chad yell.

"Come on, Lisa! You can do it!" Stevie screamed.

She pointed the nozzle higher. It didn't work.

"Higher!" Chad yelled again. Then she understood what she had to do.

She leaned forward, almost resting on Penny's neck, pointed the squirt gun into the air, well above her target, and squeezed with all her might. The blue dye arced into the air and landed—square on the target. She did it!

"Yahoo!" she yelled, turning Penny around and heading back to the starting line.

The Clubs were neck and neck with the Diamonds, and the Spades were close behind. There wasn't a second to lose. Stevie bolted off the starting line like a greyhound, and handled her part like a pro. She returned a few seconds later, grinning and triumphant. It was Carole's turn.

Lisa thought she could breathe easy now. She was sure they'd won. Almost every eye in the place was on Carole, since she was such a good rider. Lisa, however, thought that it might pay to watch Veronica diAngelo, the Diamonds' captain, two lanes over.

Veronica and Carole left the starting line at almost the same instant. They arrived at the shooting line simultaneously. They took aim together. The yellow streams of dye shot out together. Because it was such a light color, it was hard to see it land, but Lisa had the distinct impression that Veronica had missed the target. Veronica turned her pony around right away, though, and headed back to the finish line. But Carole's first shot missed. She took careful aim, shot again, and this time, hit the target.

Hard as she tried, and fast as she rode, she couldn't beat Veronica back to the starting line. That meant they'd come in second and the Diamonds had won for the day. The Spades came in right behind the Clubs in the fourth race. The Hearts were last.

The Diamonds' families and friends were cheering them on. Then the Saddle Club's own families and friends were yelling like crazy. Even Lisa's parents were cheering. Second place wasn't bad. It kept them in the competition. But it wasn't as good as first.

Kate and Red went out to pick up the targets. Lisa noticed that Kate examined the Diamonds' target, and waved to Red to join her. He walked over and looked at it, too. Then, the two of them took the target over to the judges' table. There was a lot of buzzing and chatting there. The judges spent time looking at their charts and looking at the target.

The P.A. system crackled to life. "Ladies and gentlemen," the head judge said. "We have a correction to make on the final race. A close examination of the targets reveals that one of the riders on the Diamond team did not, in fact, hit the target. Therefore, the team is automatically disqualified and comes in fourth. The new order for the final race is: Clubs, Spades, Hearts, and Diamonds. The final point standing for the day is: Clubs, thirteen; Diamonds; eleven; Hearts, nine; and Spades, seven. Teams, please line up for the presentation of ribbons."

They'd won! Lisa had been right when she'd thought Veronica hadn't hit the target. Good old Veronica had tried to cheat and she'd been caught at it!

The Clubs' ponies stood still and proud as the judges pinned the blue ribbons on their bridles. It was as if they knew what they'd done and were as proud as their riders. Lisa leaned forward to admire the shiny blue satin. She decided then that it would be the first of many, many blue ribbons she would win in her life as a rider. She glanced at her best friends. The big smiles on their faces told her they all felt exactly the same way.

It seemed to Lisa then that it almost didn't matter if they won the next two days of the gymkhana. Winning the first day was almost wonderful enough for a lifetime. Almost.

12

IT TURNED OUT to be a good thing Lisa wasn't set on winning on the second day, because they didn't.

"The best part of today was the cross-country jumping," Stevie said as the team and Kate sat at a booth at TD's, The Saddle Club's favorite hangout. It was an ice cream store at the local shopping center. They'd bought themselves sundaes as consolation prizes, since they had come in second to Veronica's Diamond team.

"Don't be too hard on yourselves," Kate advised them. "You sure looked like you were having fun out there."

"Well, we were," Stevie said. "But winning is more fun."

"Oh, I don't know," Kate said.

For the first time, Carole had the feeling that Kate

was ready to reveal some of the problems she had had with riding.

"How do you mean that?" Carole asked her.

Kate was quiet for a time, apparently thinking about her answer. The girls and Chad waited with her.

"I think," she began hesitantly, "that having fun is more important than winning. I've done a lot of winning, riding champion horses. But I think I've forgotten how to have fun. I've had more fun watching you the last few days than I had riding for a year!"

"Even when I ended up dumping an entire glass of water on you in the water race?" Stevie asked.

"Well, I might make an exception there," Kate admitted with a grin. "But I had an awful lot of fun watching Carole's pony circle the target so much in pin-the-tail-on-the-pony that she ended up putting her tail on the Spades' pony!"

"At least it was a bull's-eye," Carole said.

"Yeah, that the Spades got credit for," Chad reminded her.

"Let's face it, team," Lisa said. "Today was not our finest hour as riders."

"But that's what I mean," Kate said. "Sure, you didn't do as well as you did yesterday, but you were having *fun*! You were cracking up the entire time!"

"Were they *all* laughing when I fell off Half Dollar trying to reach Veronica's shadow in shadow tag?" Chad asked.

"Yeah—but you were laughing, too," Kate said.

"The thing you were all doing—which I had completely forgotten to do—is having *fun*. Red ribbon, blue ribbon, no ribbon at all. What does it really matter as long as you do your best and laugh a little—or a lot, if you can?"

"But if you kept winning, why weren't you having fun?" Carole asked her.

"Because—and I've only just realized it—all I cared about was the winning. When you ride in those shows, you see a lot of the same riders almost every week. You have a lot of common interests with them and they become friends—or at least they should. I got to the point where I couldn't be friends at all. All I cared about was whether I drew a position right after somebody the judges might think was better than I was, or if one of the other riders might get a muddy smudge on her boot so the judge would mark her down. Or sometimes I'd hope for a rainy day. A lot of the other horses didn't like competing in the rain." Kate paused for a minute and the full weight of what she'd said seemed to sink in for herself. She scrunched her nose in distaste. "See what I mean? Now that I think about it, it's no wonder I wasn't having any fun."

Carole spoke first. "When I read about you and met you, all I could think about was how wonderful it must be to be so good!"

"For some people, maybe," Kate said. "But it's like the better I got, the worse *it* got. The *it* was my own attitude."

"Maybe the problem isn't really riding," Carole said.

"Oh, yes it is," Kate corrected her. "Just like I explained."

"But don't you see? It's not the riding you don't like—it's the high-pressure competition. That's what turned it sour for you."

"That's right," Stevie piped in, realizing that this was just the chance The Saddle Club needed to convince Kate to start riding again. "If you stop riding, you're throwing away something you're really good at. All you really need to do is to stop competing—just ride for fun!"

"Like ride in the gymkhana tomorrow?" Kate asked, a touch of sarcasm in her voice. "It's a little late for that, isn't it?"

"It may be too late for the rest of us, too," Chad said. The girls looked to him for an explanation. He raised his left arm above the level of the table. "Remember how I fell off my pony in shadow tag? I think I really did something to my wrist."

At first, they couldn't see the problem, but on closer examination, it was very clear that Chad's whole wrist was terribly swollen. "I can't bend it much, either," he said. "It was okay for a while, but I don't know about tomorrow."

Kate reached across the table for Chad's arm. "I've seen an awful lot of bumps and bruises over the years, and this really hurts, doesn't it?" Chad tried to shrug it off, but he clearly winced when Kate touched it, even gently. "Lisa, go ask at the counter if we can have some ice in a plastic bag. That swelling's got to come down. It doesn't look like it's broken, but it sure is sprained. There's no way you can ride tomorrow, Chad. Why didn't you say something before?"

"I want our team to win, and if I can't ride, we'll be disqualified! I can't do that to you guys!"

Lisa returned with the bag of ice and they wrapped it around Chad's arm with a bandanna Carole found in her back pocket. It was probably too late to reduce the swelling, at least right away, but it did help numb it so it didn't hurt so much.

"Well, that's that," Carole said. "It wasn't your fault, Chad, it could have happened to any of us, but we might as well just give Veronica and the Diamonds the blue ribbon first thing tomorrow."

"I'm not so sure about that!" Stevie said, her eyes suddenly bright.

"You look like you're up to something," Carole said, suspicious.

"Oh, I am," Stevie agreed. "We all know there's no way Chad can ride tomorrow, but that doesn't mean he couldn't do something like help with the setups at the final races, does it?"

"Great idea," Kate said. "Red and I have been running around like crazy. We could use an extra hand—no pun intended."

"That's not what I had in mind," Stevie said. "Look, our deal with Max was that we three could be on the same gymkhana team if, and only if, we took the stable's newest rider. But if the stable's newest rider *isn't* Chad, we'd still have to take that person on our team, even if maybe that rider actually had just a little bit of experience."

"Or a whole lot of experience?" Carole asked, seeing the light.

"But who else *is* there besides Chad?" Lisa asked.

"How about Kate Devine?" Stevie said.

When a great big grin crossed Kate's face, The Saddle Club girls knew they'd achieved both of their goals. They had found a way to maybe still win the blue ribbon, and, best of all, they'd found a way to get Kate to start riding again.

"Here's to tomorrow!" Lisa announced, raising a gooey spoonful of sundae in a toast.

"To victory!" Carole chimed in. Everybody joined the toast.

MAX WAS HARD to convince. At first, he wanted to disqualify the team, but when Stevie pointed out how unfair that would be, especially since they'd been the ones to make up all the games and the rules, he finally relented.

"But Kate's a championship rider," he reminded them.

"What does championship riding have to do with gymkhanas?" Carole protested. "She never got a silver cup for popping balloons—"

"Riding skills matter a lot in a gymkhana, almost as much as on a cross-country course," he said, and the girls knew it was true.

"Okay, so give us a handicap," Kate said.

"Right, our old handicap was Chad—so we can handle *anything*!" Stevie told him, grinning.

Max wrinkled his eyebrows in thought. Finally, he nodded. "Okay, you've got a deal. I'll handicap you so nobody can say I wasn't fair. Your handicap is that your start/finish line is ten feet behind everybody else's. That will do it for the three relay races scheduled for today. The first game is horseback musical chairs. For that, you all ride without stirrups, which will make it harder to get on and off the ponies."

"Boy, you sure know how to give a team a handicap!" Stevie complained.

"Yes, I do," Max said, grinning, obviously proud of his solution. "Think you can beat the odds?"

For a moment, all four girls were trying to imagine how much harder the races would be for them, but then they realized that, in a very real way, it didn't matter. They wanted to be in the gymkhana to have fun, and if they could win with their handicaps, great, but if not, they'd still enjoy trying.

"Just watch us!" Carole said. "The Clubs will come out on top, no matter how the races end."

LISA DIDN'T HAVE Carole's confidence of their success, but she knew that the main part was that they would have fun that afternoon. In the meantime, the final portion of the adult competition was wonderful to watch.

The first day, the dressage, had been a test of manners and form. The second day was an endurance test for the horse and rider, and included a cross-country race, filled with jumps, hills, water, and other types of obstacles. It had been wild and fun to watch the horses and riders manage the course. The third and final day was a test of the horse's fitness working on a small jumping course in the ring, which had to be completed in a specific amount of time. Horses weren't judged for form (though good form made for good jumps), but they were marked down for refusing jumps or knocking them down, or not finishing the course within the allotted time.

The girls watched closely, enjoying the event immensely.

"Can you do this?" Lisa whispered to Kate.

She nodded in response. "Yes, but see how intense the riders are? Did you notice the way that last rider took her time getting her horse back out of the ring? She was hanging around trying to make the next rider nervous. I used to do that kind of thing. If that's what I have to do to win, I don't want to do it anymore at all."

"I can understand that," Lisa told her. "But I'm glad you've decided to ride with us today."

"So am I," Kate said, and smiled at her.

AT EXACTLY FOUR o'clock, the final day of the gymkhana began. Max explained to the crowd what had happened to Chad the day before. The girls were only a little annoyed when Chad insisted on stepping into the center of the ring to show everybody that his arm was in a sling. Anybody who cared to could see that while he was standing off to the side next to Red.

"That's just like Chad," Stevie said philosophically. Lisa was pleased to see that Stevie seemed resigned to letting Chad be Chad. After all, even though he wasn't the boy of her dreams, he *had* cared enough to compete as well as he could, even though he wasn't very good. There was something to be said for that.

When Max finished his explanation of the handicap system for the Clubs, the girls removed the stirrups from their ponies' saddles. Lisa winked at Stevie as she did so, remembering, now without any anger, her first day at Pine Hollow, when Stevie had saddled her horse without stirrups as a joke. Lisa hadn't thought it was very funny then. Today, with a pony, it was going to be a little funny—she hoped. With some difficulty, she mounted Penny.

All sixteen of the riders got in a circle around the chairs in the ring and the music began.

The ponies trotted to the music. At the second it stopped, each rider dismounted quickly and ran for a chair. The game was exactly the same as the old birthday-party standby, except that they were on ponyback as they circled.

All of the Clubs got chairs for the first four rounds. In fact, they discovered that Max's handicap for them on this race was no handicap at all. They just slid out of their saddles—even more quickly than their opponents. If it hadn't been for the fact that Veronica had grabbed a chair and pulled it away from Lisa before she could sit on it, they'd have won. Since nobody called a foul on Veronica, and the Clubs were in no mood to make a fuss about anything, they let the Diamonds take first place, and satisfied themselves with second.

The second race was called charades. Each rider rode to the far end of the ring, dismounted, then pulled a piece of paper with a movie title on it out of a hat. She then had to do a charade of the title. As soon as her teammates guessed the title, the rider remounted and returned to the starting line and the second rider began.

It was wild. The Clubs had no trouble with *Star Wars* and *The Karate Kid*—Lisa pretended to shoot at stars, and Stevie did two karate kicks—but Kate had a terrible time getting them to say *National Velvet,* until she began patting the soft black velvet of her riding hat. Carole got them to come up with *High Noon* quickly by pointing to her watch and then to the sky, so they ended up in second place. The good news was that the Diamonds got totally stuck on *Black Beauty* and came in third, so the Clubs were now tied for the day with their serious competition.

The third race was a balloon-popping race, and in this one, being an extra ten feet behind the start/finish line really was a handicap. Each rider got a stick with a tack on the end of it. They were to ride to the far end of the ring and pop one balloon each on a target board. Each of the Clubs did it perfectly, but so did a lot of the other riders, and the fact that the Clubs had to ride farther made them come in third. They would have been last except that one of the Spades' ponies got spooked by the long stick and wouldn't behave. That was something for the Clubs to be grateful for.

When the final race began, the score stood at Hearts, six; Spades, seven; Clubs, eight; and Diamonds, nine. That meant that it was actually possible for any team but the Hearts to win. The last race was the egg race and it was the toughest race of all—especially for the Clubs.

Stevie recalled all the smashed hard-boiled eggs their practices had cost them. It was small consolation that the team member who had been the worst at it was Chad. None of them was very good. She'd just had fun ragging Chad about his mistakes. Also, this was a race in which their ten-foot handicap was really going to matter, since it meant they'd have to balance a raw egg on a spoon for ten more feet than any of the other riders.

Mrs. Reg released her bandanna. At the instant it hit the ground, Lisa was off! She nudged Penny into a gallop and dashed to the far end of the arena. Holding Penny still with her legs, she balanced a raw egg on a tablespoon, which she held in her right hand. As soon as she was sure she had it securely, she nudged Penny gently. It wouldn't do at all to have Penny spurt as she turned, because that would unbalance the egg. Penny took her signal instantly. And spurted. *Splat.* The egg landed on the turf, a slimy yellow-and-white mess. Lisa returned to the egg bucket to get a replacement. Once. it was in the spoon, she barely touched Penny's belly, and the pony began walking. Much better. A trot would be no good at all—unless she could teach the egg to post! By using alternate leg aids, which meant touching her calves to alternating sides of Penny's stomach as the pony walked, Lisa got her to extend her walk and therefore cover more ground in less time. It took a long time, but it took a lot less time than returning for a third egg.

Happily, she handed the spoon over to Stevie. Her job was to return the egg to the bucket and then hand over the empty spoon to Carole. The final leg of the race would have Kate returning the last egg to the bucket.

Lisa was feeling proud of herself when she gave the egg to Stevie. She'd made it with only one broken egg. *Not bad*, she thought, until she saw that two of the other teams were well on their way to finishing their second legs in the time it had taken her to complete one!

At least Stevie did her job smoothly. It would have been more than she could have stood to do badly on the race she'd given her brother such a hard time about. The only trouble she had was that when she put the egg back into the bucket, it broke, smearing gooey white and yolk over the other eggs there. At first, Stevie thought this was bad news, but then she realized it might, just might, make the other eggs a little sticky. And if the other eggs were a little sticky, they might stay on the spoons a little better.

She reversed Nickel's direction and raced him back to their finish line, practically slamming the spoon into Carole's hand. Breathing hard from excitement and hard riding, she looked around. The Hearts' third rider had left at about the same time Carole had. The Diamonds were a split second behind—and they didn't have to ride as far as Carole and Kate did, but Carole and Kate were the best riders in the ring. Would it make the difference? Would the slimy eggs help or hurt?

The second question was the first one answered. The eggs were so gooey that Carole could hardly hold one in her fingers, much less get it onto the spoon! After three tries, she finally succeeded. Carole turned Quarter around, holding the spoon firmly in her hand. She got him into a walk, the pace all the riders had discovered was by far the safest, and then, answering Stevie's question about whether being a good rider would make a difference, Carole brought Quarter into a trot. She leaned forward in what was called jump position, letting her knees flex with the pony's movement. As a result, her upper body was almost motionless—and so was the egg!

She slowed Quarter down just enough to hand the spoon and egg to Kate and then joined Lisa and Stevie in their wild cheering. All of the teams were now on their final legs and all of them were close. The Diamonds had caught up with the Hearts, and Veronica was riding her very best. She'd seen Carole's trick about using jump position and did it herself, as did Kate. Kate and Veronica were practically neck and neck.

Then, the Clubs heard what they thought might be the most wonderful sound in the world. It was the sound of a raw egg hitting turf and breaking, smashing, oozing, and gooing. It was the sound of Veronica diAngelo's egg. That meant Veronica had to take an egg from the bucket and start all over again on her leg of the race.

Kate slid her egg into the bucket, turned Half Dollar around, and galloped to the finish line, grinning like she'd just won the Kentucky Derby!

The Clubs shouted and screamed with joy. They'd come in first in the final race, guaranteeing them the blue ribbon for the day, and the overall blue ribbon for the gymkhana, since they'd won two out of three days.

It wasn't easy hugging one another while they were sitting on ponies, but they managed somehow. And somehow Chad managed to get in on the yelling and cheering, even though he couldn't do much hugging with his arm in a sling.

Victory was sweet.

14

IT WASN'T HARD to talk Stevie's parents into letting the team come over to her house for a celebration pool party for the first-place gymkhana team. The Lakes agreed to let them order pizza, and once they'd settled on all the things they wanted on it (everything but anchovies, one half with no mushrooms, the other half with no green peppers), they changed into bathing suits and sat on towels around the backyard pool. When they were relaxed, gratefully sipping ice-cold glasses of lemonade and iced tea, they began to talk about Subject Number One: horses.

"I think my favorite part was when I finally got that sticky, gooey egg onto my spoon," Carole said, dangling her feet in the cool water.

"My favorite part was when I heard Veronica drop

her egg," Stevie said, standing up. "It sounded like—
this!" She performed a perfect cannonball into the
water.

"As much as I dislike wishing other people bad luck
at horse shows," Kate admitted, wiping splashes of
water off her sunglasses with her towel, "I kind of liked
that, too." She glanced over at Carole and giggled.

"*C'mon*, you guys!" Stevie said, jumping up and
down in the water. "This feels great—especially after
getting all hot and sweaty from riding." She swam over
to where Carole was sitting and tried to pull her in.

"I think I'll stay here," Carole said, using her feet to
splash Stevie. Kate grinned at them both.

Lisa slipped gracefully into the water. "I liked it when I
got you all to say *Star Wars* in the charade race."

"That was a neat race," Carole said. "I'm really glad
you thought it up," she told Lisa.

"That wasn't my idea," Lisa said. "It was yours."

"It was?" Carole asked in surprise. "I don't remember that."

"When you've been working so closely together that
you can't distinguish one person's ideas from another's," Kate said, "then you know you've *really* got a
team."

"Speaking of teams, where's Chad?" Carole asked.
"He should be here celebrating with us. It's his victory,
too. Max gave him a blue ribbon today along with
ours."

"He *should* be here—and it would be fun to have

him around—but it seems that he's totally out of horseback riding," Stevie said. She did a few hand-stands in the water, then climbed out of the pool and flopped on her towel.

"And he doesn't even want pizza with us?" Lisa asked. She pulled herself out of the pool as well.

"Nope," Stevie said. "See, while he was doing all those setups at the gymkhana, he spotted Betsy Cavanaugh's older sister in the cheering section. I think he's in love—*again*. Sorry, Lisa," she added with a giggle. "I think he's definitely off horses for good."

"That's good, but what's he onto?" Carole asked with a grin.

"He doesn't know it yet, but you all know Betsy's sister April, right?"

Carole and Lisa nodded and then began giggling.

"What's the joke?" Kate asked, turning over on her towel.

"The joke's on Chad," Carole explained. "April is really nice and very talented, but if Chad wants to take up what interests her the same way he took up horse-back riding for Lisa, it's going to be a big challenge to him."

"How's that?" Kate asked, still confused.

"April is a *ballet* dancer," Stevie explained. "And Chad's going to look silly in a leotard—especially with his arm in a sling!"

All four girls began laughing at the image of Chad trying to be a dancer!

Just then, Stevie's brother Alex appeared at the poolside with the pizza, which had been delivered. They thanked him and quickly shooed him away. "It was some trick to figure out exactly which ingredients had to go on which side of this," Carole said, admiring their work, and reaching for a piece from the non-green-pepper side.

"It's a breeze when you're good at teamwork," Kate said, returning to a subject Carole wanted to talk about some more.

"Speaking of teamwork," Carole said, leaning back on the towel and taking a bite of pizza. "Now that you're riding again, we have a team we'd like you to join permanently. Would you like to join The Saddle Club?"

"Great idea!" said Lisa.

"Oh, yes!" Stevie agreed. "You'll just love it when you ride more at Pine Hollow. And we have our meetings about once a week, but it's all pretty informal. All you have to be is horse crazy, and we know you're that."

"There's something I haven't told you guys," Kate said. "I'd love to join your club, but only if you've got out-of-town memberships."

"Oh, no!" Carole said dejectedly.

"*What?*" Stevie and Lisa said together. "I thought you'd decided to stay here," Lisa added.

"It's a transfer, isn't it?" Carole continued. "Dad was wondering why your father was being so funny about whether you would buy a house here. I guess that means that the Marine Corps has got some other bright ideas about where you all should live. And if I know the Corps, it's not Hawaii!" Carole joked.

"No, it's not. Actually, it's not even the Corps. Dad came to Quantico because he wants to retire. He's been talking to the brass about it. Two months ago, he and Mom made a down payment on a dude ranch out west. They both like horses and thought it would be perfect for me—until I ruined it by deciding to stop riding!"

Suddenly, everything that had happened at her first meeting with the Devines at Quantico a few weeks before became clear to Carole. She understood why the Devines had been so evasive about their plans. And she and her dad had thought it was because it was top secret stuff!

"But you've solved the problem now, haven't you?" Carole asked. "You've rediscovered what's *fun* about riding."

"*I* didn't solve the problem," Kate said. "*You* did—all three of you. That shows the power of good friends."

"I'm not so sure about that," Carole said, finishing a mouthful of pizza. "Personally, I don't think it's friend power, I think it's *horse* power."

"Could be!" Kate agreed. Lisa and Stevie laughed at Carole's joke.

"You know, I've always wanted to go to a dude ranch for a visit," Carole said. "I know it's very different from the kind of riding we do at Pine Hollow, but horses are horses and I bet it would be great. Will you write to us and tell us all about it?"

"I'll do better than that," Kate said. "I'll invite you all out to be our guests after it opens."

"Now *that's* horse power!" Carole declared.

"Hmm," Stevie said. "Maybe we could plan a gymkhana for the Devines' ranch. Wouldn't that be fun?"

"Only if we can have Kate on our team!" Lisa declared.

And they all agreed that would be perfect.

BONNIE BRYANT is the author of more than twenty books for young readers, including the best-selling novelizations of *The Karate Kid* movies. The Saddle Club books are her first for Bantam Books. She wrote her first book six years ago and has been busy at her word processor ever since. (For her first three years as an author, Ms. Bryant was also working in the office of a publishing company. In 1986, she left her job to write full-time.)

Whenever she can, Ms. Bryant goes horseback riding in her hometown, New York City. She's had many riding experiences in the city's Central Park that have found their way into her Saddle Club books—and lots which haven't!

The author has two sons, and they all live together in an apartment in Greenwich Village that is just too small for a horse.